LAPRISHA PADDIO

D1129072

A TREACHEROUS GAME

STREET DECEPTIONS

outskirtspress
DENVER, COLORADO

This is a work of fiction. The events and characters described herein are imaginary and are not intended to refer to specific places or living persons. The opinions expressed in this manuscript are solely the opinions of the author and do not represent the opinions or thoughts of the publisher. The author has represented and warranted full ownership and/or legal right to publish all the materials in this book.

A Treacherous Game
Street Deceptions
All Rights Reserved.
Copyright © 2012 Laprisha Paddio
v2.0

Cover Photo © 2012 JupiterImages Corporation. All rights reserved - used with permission.

This book may not be reproduced, transmitted, or stored in whole or in part by any means, including graphic, electronic, or mechanical without the express written consent of the publisher except in the case of brief quotations embodied in critical articles and reviews.

Outskirts Press, Inc.
http://www.outskirtspress.com

ISBN: 978-1-4327-9135-3

Outskirts Press and the "OP" logo are trademarks belonging to Outskirts Press, Inc.

PRINTED IN THE UNITED STATES OF AMERICA

Prologue

Twenty years in age and a new breed of young hustlers was on the prowl. Fresh out of high school and holding, on the block, posted up trying to get their grind on were two of Chicago's worst nightmare youngsters that quickly earned a name for themselves in the streets; running from the near north side of the Chi, serving all types of fiends from the wealthy to the poor.

It was the summer time and hot, Khalik, Hassan, and Jose, who were all young and full of hostility and vigor, drove around in Jose's old school Chevy that Jose's uncle gave him for his eighteenth birthday.

"Damn its probably 'bout 2:00 in the morning and we're riding around with not a damn thing to do," Khalik said, with his eyes glassy and nearly closed, taking a few extra puffs before he passed the joint to Hassan, who was sitting in the back seat. Hassan was dazed from the weed they had been smoking; not to mention the lines of cocaine sniffed into his nose, sending him into an ultimate high. Shortly before he met up with Khalik and Jose, he had consumed two straight shots of Hennessy, which did not help.

"What time is it?" Khalik asked, answering his own question as he looked up at the time on the car radio that read 2:30. His vision was slightly clouded. He blinked a few times so that he could see a little better. "Damn, I feel like I'm about to pass out. Jose, pull up in that alley right there and park." As Jose pulled into the alley and parked Khalik started to think. He thought of how every time he would pass through that same alley, there would be a car that caught his interest. *I wonder if that motherfucker is going to ride through here tonight.* He thought to his self. "Yo, check it, we're going to rob us somebody tonight." He said out of the clear blue. The expression on his face, as well as, the words flowing from his tongue grew attention.

"Who," Hassan looked up at Khalik with the joint still in his mouth with the wrinkles from his expression crunching up his forehead. He leaned forward trying to take control of his high and listen to what he was saying. "Who are you talking about Khalik?"

"This white boy I see riding around here. Every time, I come through this alley, he up in here with some trick off the street, and I know your boy caked up just from the ride he be in. Shit, he looks like he got that paper, and I don't have any problem showing him what to do with it."

"What the hell you coming through here for?" Jose looked at Khalik with his eyebrow raised and a smirk upon his face just as high as the others. "What, you be up in here trying to catch you some of that injection ass?" He said sarcastically, laughing at his own comment.

"What, injection ass, what's that?" Khalik had no idea what Jose was talking about and from the sounds of it, he was not feeling it at all.

Jose and Hassan started to laugh. "That lethal injection nigga, that one hitter quitter. These bitches got AIDS and stuff man. They got that shit that'll put your ass to sleep." Hassan laughed even harder at the thought of his boy trick in' with some prostitute in a dark alley.

"Damn man I know you not going out like that." Jose started to clown him once again.

"Fuck y'all man I'm not doing that shit." Khalik frowned at being the center of the joke. He had no problem getting with the girls. *These niggas must have forgotten who I am. I do not need to trick off as handsome as I am.* Secretly admiring his own looks in his thoughts to his self. I be coming through here to meet up with my boy sometimes. I get my shit from him, he gets his money, and I'm out. In fact, some of that same stuff you motherfuckers are smoking on now. While y'all clowning me and shit."

As ten minutes passed by, they continued to sit back and chill, still parked in the dark alley waiting; catching a deeper high from the smoke that filled the air in the car from the joint they finished more than five minutes before.

"Now tell me what we out here waiting for." Jose asked Khalik again wanting him to repeat why they were still sitting there waiting so long.

"Okay, everyday there is this same black BMW that drives through and stops over here around 2:45 in the morning like clockwork, and he always picks up this bitch. Now I'm pretty sure from the ride and the way the cracker looks that he got that paper." Khalik explained.

"So just because he got a BMW we supposed to be waiting for what?" Jose continued to ask unnecessary questions. "I mean, how we supposed to know if he's going to show up tonight? We're really just sitting here for nothing."

"Whatever, like I said the ride is right. It is a black BMW with some BBS rims and a nice system, so when he pulls up we are going to pull up beside him, Hassan, and me are going to get out, and then we are just going to rob his ass. It's as simple as that." Khalik explained his plan to them so nonchalantly. It was as if he already had it on his mind.

"So we're taking the ride and what else?" Jose became a bit confused. "I'm down for taking the shit, but I already have a car so what is this going to do to benefit me?"

Why is this motherfucker my boy? He asked his self. "What else? We're taking whatever we can get." Khalik turned around towards the back seat. "Hassan, you and I are going to get out and get this shit done as quickly as possible; I'm talking 'bout less than two minutes." The more he began to talk the more exaggerated he became, and Hassan seemed to get tired of waiting already. The effects from the cocaine left him hyped up and ready for whatever. The adrenalin was rushing through him like blood flowing through his veins.

"Fuck, man we have been waiting out here in this hot ass car for about 20 minutes already, I know it got to be passed the time for this nigga to roll through, this motherfucker not coming, let's go. What time is it anyway?" Hassan complained, tired of waiting and doing nothing.

As Jose looked at his watch, he noticed it was 2:44, "Damn, where the hell is he?"Jose expressed impatiently, when the black BMW, they were waiting for pulled up in the alley in front of the prostitutes who worked the streets nearby.

As Khalik looked up, he noticed the car pulling up nearby. "Shit, there it goes right there," He said, "Jose, pull up next to 'em." Jose started the car and turned his lights off, slowly pulling alongside of the BMW, leaned back in the seat with his eyes closed and pants unzipped being served from the prostitute he meets up with weekly, the man in the car didn't notice them pulling up alongside of them.

Khalik and Hassan both wore hoodies because of the chill in the air as they pulled their hoods over their heads getting ready to move in on the black BMW. Khalik asked Hassan, "You ready nigga?"

"Shit I'm always ready." Hassan confirmed to Khalik; reassuring him, that he was down for whatever.

"Aiight then, grab your shit and let's do this." Referring to the guns, they had in the car with them, waiting on the day they would have to pull one out and use it on one of the niggas in the street. Khalik jumped out of the car and opened the door to the driver's side of the BMW. "Give me your wallet and get the hell out of the car," He expressed while holding a black .22 caliber pistol to his head.

The man was distraught and shaken with nervousness. "Please don't shoot." He said as the prostitute muffled out a sound with his dick still in her mouth.

Hassan opened the passenger's side door placing a Beretta to the girls head "Don't make a nigga shoot your ass bitch. I'm already madder than a motherfucker, waiting on this punk ass white boy." Hassan pulled her up by her hair and dragged her out of the car, slinging her to the ground. She quickly picked herself up from the dirty street in the alley. "Aint gone be no problem is it bitch?" Pointing the gun in her face as she held on to the ground, scared.

"No there is no problem. I didn't see anything." She said to him with nervousness.

"Good, then get the fuck out of here 'for I shoot your trick ass." She slowly pulled herself up from the ground and walked off as if she had seen nothing, dusting off her tightly fitted dress that barely covered her g-string. Hassan looked at the man as if he was ready to just shoot him on the strength that he had more than Hassan had ever had in his entire life. "What the fuck you looking at?" Hassan screamed at the man with anger.

"Nothing, I'm not looking at anything." He closed his eyes and began to pray silently to his self. *Oh, God if you help me through this, I promise I will never buy another piece of ass as long as I live.*

"Open your motherfucking eyes." Hassan tapped him on the head with the gun.

Khalik could tell that the man was surprised and scared. "Look we don't have time for this man. Let's just get what we came to get and go."

"O.k. look, I'll give you what you want, just don't shoot me. You'll be making a very big mistake, and you don't want to spend the rest of your life behind bars over something like this. My father is a police officer. This would be a mistake. Whatever you want I'll get it for you, just don't shoot." He said beginning to get more nervous, staggering and stuttering his words with his dick still hanging out of his pants. He was scared that they were going to shoot him in the head he began to try to bargain with them.

"Shut the fuck up, rich ass white boy." Hassan slapped the man across the head with the gun over, and over again, only this time knocking him out cold, as his head fell unto the passenger's seat of the car gushing with blood from the gash, the gun left on the side of his head.

"Aiight, let's see what you got." Talking to the unconscious man, Khalik turned him over and searched for the wallet in his pockets.

"Bingo" He looked inside and there were 500 dollars and a gold card, along with the man's ID. "Andrew Smith." Khalik read from his ID card.

"Yeah we got your ID, and we know where you live in case you want to try something." Hassan told the still unconscious man as he pulled off his shoes. *Yeah, these are nice I can sell these on the streets. They may not be Stacy Adams, but they close enough.* He thought.

Khalik pulled the watch off his wrist and the ring off his finger. "Come on man let's go here come a car, It looks like them laws." Noticing the white car pulling into the ally, Khalik ran back to the car and jumped in the front seat.

"Wait, what? We didn't even get the car." Hassan stood in the way of the car door on the passenger's side.

"Man come on, forget the car let's go." Jose yelled out from the driver's side window.

"Fuck this motherfucker," He pushed the unconscious man lying in a small puddle of his own blood out of the car and jumped into the driver's seat, closing both doors.

"What the hell are you doing man?" Jose yelled out again to Hassan.

"Man, just go on Jose; we'll catch up with him later, go." Khalik said thinking that the car might have been the laws. Jose sped off, pulling out from the alley and left Hassan behind, who then, pulled off behind them going in the opposite direction from the white car. Driving the BMW, he sped off, leaving the man lying in the middle of the street and a mist of dust in the air from the car taking off so fast.

The nearby prostitutes stood on the street looking as they drove away, wondering what was going on. The girl whom was thrown from the car rushed over to Andrew's aid. "Are you alright?" She asked, placing her hands upon his shoulder, shaking him. She tried to awaken him from the unconscious state he was in, but he was barely moving.

Yeah, I'm going to keep this bitch for myself. I got me a new ride for these hoes now. Hassan thought to his self. He felt good. This was exactly the type of rush he needed in his life, and he liked it.

"Damn, man what's wrong with him? He is always doing something stupid. I am not going to jail for some bitch ass BMW man; just because he does not know when to chill. Damn" Jose said.

"Aiight man, he knows what he's doing." Khalik told Jose with confidence, but was really burning with anger inside from the many dumb and careless acts Hassan had done before, especially involving him, but he didn't care that was still his boy, and he had his back no matter what the consequences.

"Yeah, let's hope so. That motherfucker is loco man, straight up." Jose continued to drive down the street noticing that no one was following behind them after about 2 miles down the road, when the phone began to ring.

"That's him calling me right now. Yeah hello, Hassan? Man, what is wrong with your ass man? You're going to get us caught up messing with that damn car." Khalik said yelling into the phone and making faces as if he could see his anger. "I said let's roll. That means to forget about the car. I thought the law was coming."

"What, Nigga this was your idea in the first place, besides; I need me a ride, can't be caught up under that motherfucking Jose all the time, riding with him and shit." Hassan expressed with a bit of humor and seriousness flowing through his voice all at the same time.

"Whatever man, meet us up at the spot, at Jose's house, so we can split this dough." Khalik told Hassan.

"Fuck that shit. I got myself a BMW baby. Y'all niggas can have it. I'm tired of penny pinching anyway. Pretty soon our pockets are going to be overflowing with money, and this is only the beginning.

"Do you want your cut or not." Khalik said.

"Naw, holler at you in a minute yo," Hassan hung up. *They must think this is a game, well, not for me it's not I'm about to get mines, by any means necessary.* He thought to his self, feeling the rush from his first robbery. Hassan instantly developed more of that I don't care mentality streaming through his brain.

Chapter One

Reminisce

K halik lie quietly on the cot and what was considered to be his bed. He balled the pillow underneath his head for support, staring at the dirty white walls that he had been trapped between in the Illinois state prison for the past three years.

"Dead man walking."

As he lay there he turned his head to the sound of the words spoken from the tall guard with his pale white skin as he walked the inmate down the hallway; coming from the corridors of the death row segregation unit, passing through the halls of the inmates and minutes from a long-awaited death of execution. The thought of his last breath trembled through Khalik's mind, thinking that he could soon be on that same journey; a journey that started all too long ago, but seemed like only yesterday. With the crooked cops that put him there, even a drug charge could possibly turn into murder charges and life in prison. As he thought back to the beginning and to the very time he had committed some of his first crimes that would later be nothing, as many more would follow.

Khalik and Hassan stood posted up. "I'm gone need to re-up in a minute," Khalik told him leaning against the wall next to the gunny man store shooing off the flies surrounding his head.

"These fiends out here bad man, for real." Hassan implied looking around and peeping at the scenery."

"Shit, they can't be any better than these damn flies. Fuck this, come on let's bounce for the laws roll up around here." Khalik continued to shoo off the flies as they started to head toward him.

"Hey man you got something for me? I need something man just a little taste." Jump said, who was a former college basketball player turned fiend that was famous for his nice jump shots; walking up to Hassan and Khalik as they were walking back towards the block fidgeting and scratching at the sores embedded into his skin.

"Nigga, get the hell away from me man with your dirty ass, smelling like shit. You know I don't do anything over here. Bring your ass to the block." Hassan shoved jump out of the way.

"Goddamn man every time I see that nigga Jump, he's smelling like that. Looking all dirty and shit like he haven't taken any bath all his damn life." Khalik said as him and Hassan started to laugh. "I thought he was going to do something with his self. Damn, It's messed up how people change, being out here on these streets."

"All from one hit, damn, oh well, mo' money in my pockets." Hassan replied with that I don't give a care attitude. They walked up on the corner of the block where they spent most of their days and nights hustling; posted up on the wall. "It's hot than a bitch out here today, shit." He complained, wiping the sweat from his forehead. "What time you want to holler at Jimmy? He says he got some stuff for us out of state, but I don't know, sometimes that nigga Jimmy makes me want to his old ass, for real."

"Well, let's head over there now and get out of this heat." Khalik said feeling a little drained from the 90 degree weather they had been standing in all day long. Khalik and Hassan got into the car and drove up the Gold Coast where Jimmy lived. Getting out of the car, Khalik rang the door bell.

"Come on in Jimmy's waiting on y'all." One of Jimmy's muscle head, idiot guards said who was there for his protection if a nigga wanted to get out of line. They walked into the house looking around. "He in the office, you know where it is." Looking at them, upside their heads with his oversized arms folded across his chest.

They walked off, Hassan eyeballing the guard as he walked behind Khalik into the office where Jimmy was sitting at his desk smoking a Cuban cigar with a black Versace robe on. *Fuck you nigga, beat your motherfucking ass. Fuck you looking at like that, bitch ass.* Hassan angrily said to his self, wishing the guard could read his thoughts.

"What's good Jimmy?" Khalik asked as they walked on in the room.

Jimmy looked at them, sitting back in the oversized chair, puffing on the cigar like a mafia crime boss; and blowing smoke rings in the air. He leaned up towards the desk, with his elbows rested on the marble top. "I want you niggas to take a trip up to Alabama to get some paper from somebody that owes me some dough. He owes me 15 g's, but 20 g's, just for the added interest."

"Yo', Jimmy we don't give a fuck what we got to do to get that money, we're going to deliver it all, for real." Hassan insisted with a bit of fearlessness in his tone.

"Yeah, you know we get down for ours." Khalik added.

Jimmy's glance at the two of them one by one then leaned back into his chair, puffing the cigar once more. "Calm down, the last thing I need is some punk fucking up my money." He looked at Hassan.

"Man who the......" He said, taking off his Versace shades as he began to respond to the comment Jimmy had made, but Khalik interrupted before he could finish.

"Yeah, aiight, we got it." Khalik said, shaking his head in confirmation to Jimmy's comment.

"Good, don't make me regret it. You leave in two days so get whatever you have to do and wrap it up and have all my dough, otherwise y'all are going to have some other problems on your hands."

"Jimmy, now you know we always on top of our game old head, and we're going to be ready to ship out so don't worry." Khalik replied back.

"Yeah" Jimmy said under his breath. *Yeah right motherfucker, your ass better not fuck up my money or else.* He thought. *Look at this punk. If he wasn't so much like me when I was his age, I would've smoked his ass a long time ago. That's probably why I should have; that's the last thing I need is a young nigga trying to be me and shit.* Looking at Hassan as he approached, walking towards the desk.

"Shit, we haven't let you down any other time before." Hassan said putting on his shades and eyeballing Jimmy as they started to walk out of the door. *Forget you, all this is 'bout to be mines in a minute, the robe too.* He thought. He too had a thing for Versace. "Old ass, bitch ass nigga." He mumbled under his breath.

"Yeah little nigga just watch your mouth before I put something in it and get the job done." Jimmy said overlooking the remark he had heard, looking at them as they turned and exited the room. *I can see I'm going to have to teach him a lesson sooner or later.* Jimmy's thought to his self as he continued to smoke his cigar while leaned back in the chair. Jimmy was one of the few old school drug hustlers out on the streets. Most of the hustlers were young trying to get it and would do anything for it; for the life, the thrill, money, and woman who came along with the territory. Jimmy got word of the two and how fearless and street savvy they were, so he quickly took them under his wing; putting them out on the streets.

"Damn Khalik, man we need to start doing our own thing instead of having to pay some old head ass nigga that thinks his shit doesn't stink. He's going to make me show his ass something one of these days."

"Man, Jimmy just 'bout his paper like we are. Be patient, we're going to get it real soon, trust me." He told Hassan as they exited out of the house passing the same guard who let them in.

"Yeah man but he's always acting like we're not getting him more money than the rest of these dealers out here, hustling day and night just to pay somebody else some dough. That stuff burns me up for real."

"Whatever man, just keep your head on straight and everything is gone work out fine, exactly how we want it to; all in good time man. All this will be ours to run, and that nigga will be out of business like the rest of 'em." Khalik explained.

As they walked to the car, they hadn't realized that the guard heard everything they had mentioned. *Oh they plan on taking over some shit, huh; we'll see what Jimmy thinks 'bout that.* The guard said to his self as they left Jimmy's house. The guard walked back into the house and into Jimmy's office. "Yeah, boss, I just overheard them talking as they walked out saying they're going to own all this and get rid of you in the process."

"Is that right, well, well, looks like I might be taking care of them sooner than later." Jimmy picked up the phone to make a call. "Yeah this Jimmy, I got some young hustlers coming up there to get that 20 g's so take care of them. Khalik and Hassan, little niggas think they larger than life because I got them moving a little weight here and there. Show them what it's all about. Word is, these punks trying to take over and put me out of business. So let's see if they know how to hang with the big boys. We're gonna teach them a lesson." He hangs up the phone, smiling to himself wickedly. *Young punks, let's see what's up now.*

Jimmy had been through all the cut throat stuff the game had to offer and had his share of offing people. He knew that it would have to come to this, the day where Khalik and Hassan felt like they wanted to claim their own. It was only a matter of time. Jimmy thought long and hard about when he was at that age. How hungry he was and ready to get it no matter what the cost. The only thing he was willing to pay was another niggas life just to get the life he felt he deserved, but these days they were nothing like that. They were a bark and no bite. To Jimmy, even Khalik and Hassan didn't seem to live up to what he thought they were; they were far too soft. He needed to teach them a little lesson to show them how good they had it, and if they fucked up how quickly it can be taken away from them.

Khalik and Hassan pulled up to the Cabrini-Green Projects. They see Tre standing out in front of the building.

"What's up Tre, little dude, how you living baby?" Khalik asked his younger brother.

"Oh you know me, just keeping my hands clean and living good."

"Yeah, that's what it's about baby. Finish school and we're going to get you in Halsted Bank making that money so you can own your own bank someday. Be the big man in Chi-town."

"What's up man, are you ready to roll with the big dogs, make you some paper." Hassan asked, jokingly, throwing punches at Tre.

"Hell naw man, you know he's not gonna be doing none of that shit. Come on let's roll. Tre I'll be back in a little while. I'm going over there by Oak Street for a while to visit a few people and I'll be home shortly. You gonna be alright?" Khalik asked?

"Damn, man you act like he 12 years old or something, come on."

"Yeah, I think I'll be good for a few hours." Tre responded laughing at how hard his brother's exterior was, but also soft when it came to him; treating him like he was a baby.

Tre was younger than Khalik, and they were the only family that each other had since the passing of their mom. Tre imagined that she was in heaven watching over them. He wasn't a saint, but he didn't get his self-involved into the street life like his brother. No matter what Khalik had done it could never be too bad for him to turn his back on him; he loved his brother. His mom would be worried to death of the things going on in his life, but she would still love him just the same; never judgmental, but always accepting.

"Aiight bro, later." Khalik drove over to see this female he had been seeing for a while now. He dropped Hassan off to his car on the block before he headed out. Hassan continued to work through the night getting his paper straight. Since he already had Jimmy's money out of the way it was time to get his grind on for his self, try to make that change before they headed out to Alabama.

Damn I got to get Khalik to stop the bullshit and be more about our paper instead of Jimmy's. If we let him that old head is gone continue to disrespect us like we're not shit. I got something for these niggas though, these motherfuckers in Chi-town, and they gonna give me my respect, one way or the other. Hassan thought.

Two days later, They stepped off the plane in the Birmingham Alabama Shuttlesworth International Airport, where they had a rental car waiting for them when they arrived. They had already had instructions to call Jimmy, as soon as they landed so he can make sure they knew exactly where they needed to go. They had made previous stops in Alabama before but never in Birmingham, so they had no idea who they were meeting with or were they were going.

Khalik reached in his pocket and got out his cell phone to call Jimmy. "Yeah we're here, now what? Where are we headed to?"

"There's a guy waiting for y'all in a silver Toyota. When you hang up the phone flash your lights twice then follow him." Jimmy hung up the phone.

"He said flash the lights twice and to follow a silver Toyota." Khalik told Hassan.

"See this is the shit I'm talking 'bout. We don't even know who we're following. We're doing all this extra stuff for him, and we don't know if the laws are in that car or what. How we know if Jimmy is not setting us up or something," Hassan said with suspicion.

"Man come on, what's he gonna gain from setting us up, think about it, let's just get this over with."

"Yeah, aiight, but I'm not feeling this at all for real man." Hassan flashed the lights and followed the silver car to the Holiday Inn Hotel where the driver then got out of the car and escorted them to their room. He was a tall heavy-set man standing about 6'2 with a really dark-skinned complexion and a country accent.

He opened the door for them. "Here you boys go, just put your shit down and make your way back to the car, so we can go see my boss and don't keep me waiting 'cause I hate to wait, and you won't want to make me mad." The man walked out of the room and headed back down the stairs to the silver Toyota. Soon after, Khalik and Hassan followed behind him getting into their rental car.

They pulled up to an abandoned building, and they all got out of their cars. "Where the fuck we at man?" Hassan demanded, talking to the tall man who escorted them to their room. "Why the hell you riding in a Toyota?" He chuckled lightly to his self.

"Chill out. We don't know anything 'bout these niggas or what they 'bout to do, chill wit' the jokes." Khalik said peeping out the scenery.

The man looked at Hassan upside his head, but didn't respond to the comment. "We're here to meet Bama, my boss, so straighten up; you don't want to make a bad first impression, now do you?" Bama was supposed to be a well-known dealer in the streets of Birmingham. He had a few of his boys standing behind him as Khalik and Hassan walked into the door of the abandoned building.

"Well, well, I guess you two are the little boys I've been hearing about. It looks like a bunch of young punks if you ask me." They all started to laugh except for Khalik and Hassan.

"Look, I will bust a…" Hassan began to get upset.

Khalik quickly interrupted his words, holding him back, "Just give us what we came to get, and we'll be on our way."

"Yeah, well, I will get that for you when ever I feel like you deserve it, but right now Big Show and my boys are going to show you how we get down in Bama, hell you might even get you a little pussy if you're lucky. Meanwhile, you better keep that dog on a leash before he gets put to sleep. Now get the fuck out of my face."

Khalik and Hassan started to walk out of the building with Big Show following behind them. "Man I'm telling you this isn't right, these country ass niggas treating us like we shit on the ground or something."

"Just be cool and let's do what we came to do and by tomorrow, we'll be up out of here." Khalik said.

"So you boys think you can handle the great life, huh?" Big Show said walking towards them from behind.

"Look, just give us the bread, and I won't bust your ass." Hassan said with an expression of anger on his face walking back up to Big Show, who was twice his size.

"Is that what you gone do?" Big Show punched him in the face and started to kick him as he was folded on the ground. Two of Bama's boys came from behind grabbing Khalik, holding him back as one of the other men continued punching him in his stomach. Finally, after several minutes of them taking a beating the boys let Khalik go, throwing him onto the ground. Big Show stopped the stomping to Hassan's entire abdomen and side, while he lied on the ground, balled up.

"Now next time we see you, it won't be any lip. Bama is expecting you to be back here at 10:00 tomorrow morning so do not be late. In the meantime, go to your hotel and get you some rest, clean your selves up; looking like shit." Show adjusted his clothes and walked out of the building with the guys following behind him.

Bama followed behind, um, um, um, you boys are going to learn yet. By the time I get through with you you'll be good as new. He told them with his well-spoken country accent; sounding as if he was from the south, but without the street talk.

"Fuck man, I knew this shit was faulty." Lifting his head from the ground where he lay while Big Show kicked him repeatedly. "We're going to get these niggas Khalik. Jimmy set this up; I bet he did. Why else are these country motherfuckers going to take us to an abandoned building and kick the shit out of us, huh?"

"I don't know, but you're right." Khalik said to Hassan pulling up from the ground. "Let's just get the hell out of here for right now before they come back with some guns or something." As they both got up from the ground, they headed towards the door of the building and got into the car. Khalik slowly hopped into the driver's seat and started to drive off; using only one hand to steer with. His other arm was in pain from getting thrown onto the ground.

As they drove back to the Holiday Inn Hotel, which was only minutes away from where they were and Khalik had remembered the way, they were both silent. After five minutes of riding Hassan asked out of nowhere. "Khalik man when is the last time you talked to Tanya?" Sometimes he was funny like that. No matter what happened, Hassan could turn on a smile just as quick as he could a frown. Either way you never knew what he was thinking. However, he was always real with Khalik.

"Fuck that bitch." Khalik responded angrily. He was already mad, but the thought of that name made him even angrier. "Why you're bringing up old shit anyway. I mean, we're sitting here banged up and all you can think about is some bitch."

"Awe man, I was just wondering, shit I got to think about something else besides how I'm going to kill these country ass niggas. Besides, I've been meaning to ask you I just didn't get around to it. This situation just reminded me of when we set that nigga Caine up and them bitches was there. But I guess we can't call anybody out in this motherfucker, but I got them country boys though. They're going to see me.

"Yeah I do remember that shit man, that was crazy." Although they had been badly beaten and in a grimy situation, they laughed as they reminisced about that night.

Khalik's phone continues to ring, vibrating through on his waist. As he got into the BMW to drive off his phone rang again. It was Hassan. He answered, "Yeah, what up?"

"What's up man, Jimmy wants us to make a little run over there and see what Caine up to. He says the nigga been coming up short on the paper, he owes him, about 50 g's. So he wants us to check it out.

You know, scope him for a little while."

"So we just supposed to sit around peeping him out, or he wants us to get his paper?" Khalik asked.

"Oh yeah, he wants his money. He was sure about that, but he also wants us to just peep out his moves.

"Aiight, well I'm headed back now so I'll be there shortly."

"Aiight bet"

Hassan hung up the phone and dialed Darell's number.

"Yeah what up?"

"What you up to D?" Hassan asked.

"Who is this?" Darrell questioned.

"This Hassan, what's good? What are y'all doing around there?"

"Shit nothing just chilling out here tripping of this nigga Caine."

"Oh yeah, Caine out there. What that nigga up to, he out there showboating and shit?" Hassan inquired.

"Yeah, you know Caine man."

"Who the fuck is that?" Caine yelled out from the background.

"This is Hassan man chill with all that yelling all in my ear and shit." Darrell said.

"Yeah tell his punk ass I said what's up. Ask that motherfucker why they not out here wit' us? I guess they too busy up Jimmy's ass all day." Caine continued with the disrespect while puffing on a blunt.

Yeah bitch ass nigga, He thought. "Man forget all that, look; we headed out that way; that's the reason I called so try to keep that motherfucker out there for a while. I got something for his ass. Naw you know what, make sure his ass gets twisted if you can. I got something for him, fa' show."

"Well what up? You know I'm in cause I'm 'bout two minutes away from sprawling a nigga out." Darrell said, getting sick of Caine's mouth.

"Just keep him out there. It's gonn be a while, but I'll be there. You know I got you though." Hassan assured him.

"Aiight." Darrell hung up with Hassan. He stood with his back up against the building, puffing on the blunt and watching Caine's every move. He took another puff and passed it to Caine.

"Man what Hassan want?" He asked as he took the blunt from Darrell.

"Oh, you know, just shooting the shit."

"Fuck his punk ass, him and Khalik been acting like some bitches. Them young motherfuckers been running for Jimmy, and they act like they forget who done taught they ass how to get down. I mean, I have been rolling with Jimmy long before they were around, and he's treating me like I'm any old nigga off the street. They got me fucked up, all of 'em. Treating me like I'm not shit and think I'm not getting mine; they out of their minds." He continued to puff on the blunt before passing it to one of the other guys hanging out on the corner.

Darrell picked up the bottle that sat on the ground next to him and began to take a sip from it.

"What's that you drinking on?" Caine asked.

"Oh you are not ready for this shit right here. You know I keep it old school." He said trying Caine 'cause he knew how much he hated for someone to think he was weak.

Whatever, man let me get some of that." He grabbed the bottle from Darrell and read the label. "Wild Turkey, nigga this is whiskey. Man don't nobody drink this."

"I told you I wasn't ready so don't play with my drink nigga. If you're not gonna drink it give it back."

Caine looked at the full bottle. "Whisky huh, this is aiight. I might as well take me a few swig's man since there isn't anything else going on out here. Aint no hoes 'round." He took a sip from the bottle. "Damn, this shit got some kick to it for real." He cleared his throat trying to get past the burning sensation running down into his chest. "Yeah that's aiight though."

Khalik picked up Hassan and headed to North Halsted Street heading towards South of North Avenue called the SoNo neighborhood where Caine sat out with Darrell and some others on the corner. They pulled up and parked down on the street three cars back from Caines. Hassan picked up his phone and called Darrell. "Hey, we out here just sit tight for a minute, and I'm gone hit you back when we ready and let you know what's up."

"Who was that?" Khalik asked.

"That was D. I was on the phone wit' him after I got off with you and come to find out this dude Caine out there talking a lot of mess. I mean if I didn't hear it wit' my own two ears, I'd swear somebody was lying if they told me that."

"Oh yeah"

"Yeah, but I got something for his ass though."

"Aiight bet, what's up?" Khalik asked.

"We're gonna get Jimmy his money, but we're gonna get us something too. You feel me, we're gonna set his bitch ass up."

Khalik began to laugh. "You know I'm with it. I don't like that motherfucker anyway."

The fiend walked up towards Caine pulling his change from out his pocket. "Hey man I need me a little to hold me over for the night." He said.

"What!" Caine yelled out to the fiend.

"You know; I just need a little something until tomorrow. Later, I'll take care of you and then some." He continued while standing in front of Caine fidgeting.

"Look, either you're gonna buy the shit or your gonna get the fuck from out my face yo."

"Awe man, all I got is two dollars and a little change on me right now man, come on brother you know I'm good for it. I thought I was your best customer man."

"Best customer, man get out of here with that. You think I give a fuck 'bout that. You aint nothing but a fiend, and if you aint buying then get the fuck from 'round here." Caine turned his back towards the fiend.

"Come on man don't do me like that." He placed his hand on Caine's shoulder.

Caine looked back and brushed his hand away "Nigga, don't ever put your fucking hands on me. I ought to kill your ass."Then he slapped him so hard he fell to the ground. "Get your punk ass out of here." He kicked him in the side of his ribs and spat on him as he lay on the ground. All the guys who stood out on the corner laughed.

"Damn Caine, you didn't have to do him like that." The man screamed out.

"Gimme them two dollars bitch." He said to the fiend, then snatched the two dollars from his hands and kicked him once more. "Now get up and get your ass out of here."The man rose up and quickly ran off.

"Look at this motherfucker man. This man is all outside bringing attention to his self. Look at 'em." Hassan said to Khalik.

"Shit. Look at his neck and wrist, he's iced out. You know he's not pushing that much since Jimmy cut his ass down." Khalik responded as they watched Caine make a fool of his self.

"Yeah that's where Jimmy's money at right there. Damn man, he got to be one of the stupidest people I know, or he just doesn't give a fuck. I mean he's stealing Jimmy's money, coming up short, and he not even trying to hide it; the nigga blinging."

Khalik and Hassan continued to sit in the car and watch as Caine rant and raved on, bragging about how long his money was. After about an hour Caine decided to end his night hustling on the street corner.

"Damn man this Wild Turkey is a strong. Look here, I'm gonna catch y'all tomorrow. I'm 'bout to head home." Caine dapped up the guys hanging out on the corner with then turned towards Darrell and clasped his hands. "Aiight man, I'll holler at you."

"You good man, you need a ride home? You straight?" Darrell asked trying to see how tipsy he really was.

"Yeah, I'm good." He looked at him, and Darrell could see how glassy his eyes were. He walked over towards the car staggering before finally getting in his Lexus. He pulled out of the parking lot and began to drive off.

As Khalik and Hassan pulled off following behind him, Hassan picked up the phone and called Darrell. "Aiight D we 'bout to follow him home, is he wasted or what?"

"Yeah, he out there bad man," Darrell responded. "What's up though, are you good?"

"Yeah man, call some of the goons and have 'em come out to Caine's in about 20 minutes. Tell 'em to make sure they come prepared and unidentified." He said making sure they came strapped and with hoodies on.

"Aiight bet"

"Aiight." Hassan hung up the phone after confirming with Darrell. "Khalik, man I need you to call Tonya and get her and her girl over here in about 20 minutes and meet up at Caine's house."

Khalik picked up the phone and called Tanya. "What up, you down to make a little money?" He asked her.

"Shit yeah, what a bitch got to do?" She replied.

"You know Caine right?"

"Yeah I know that crazy motherfucker, why?" She asked.

"Well, meet me up at his crib in about 20 minutes and stay low key." He explained to her as they continued following Ciane.

Ten minutes passed, and Hassan and Khalik pulled up to Lakeshore Drive and parked just far back enough behind Caine's Lexus to stay out of sight.

"Aiight, we're gonna sit back for a minute and wait until they all get here, then we're gonna make our move."

It was pitch black out and the streets were hardly lit up with streetlights, only headlights from cars passing through. Caine parallel parked in between two cars barely making it; parking crooked. He stepped out of the car and engaged the security lock when he closed the door. Drunk and staggering from all the liquor settled into his bloodstream, Caine fidgeted with the keys a little as he walked towards the door. "Damn, that was strong. I'm fucked up." He spoke aloud to his self.

Just then, an SUV pulled up and parked on the opposite side of the street. Hassan rolled down the window and looked over at the car to see one of Darrell's boys sticking his head out of the window and giving him a nod.

"Aiight, they're here." Hassan told Khalik.

Khalik's phone rang. "Yeah, aiight pull over and park." Khalik hung up the phone. "Tonya and her girl here."

Hassan got out the car and walked over to Tonya's ride. He gave them the game plan and then headed toward the SUV. After piecing everything together Hassan walked back to the car. "Aiight man we're gonna stay right here for a second. I got Tonya and her girl going to the door like the car ran out of gas or running hot or something. Those niggas are going to get out when I signal them to go get his ass."

Tonya and Ebony stepped out of her car and began walking towards the front door of Caine's house. Tonya rang the doorbell several times before Caine came to the door.

"Yeah, who is it?" He yelled out from behind the closed door.

"Ciane, it's me Tonya. Open up my car ran out of gas, and I need to use your phone." She yelled back.

Caine opened the door. He looked at them both from head to toe and asked, "Where you're phone at and why the fuck you ringing my door bell like you the laws or something?"

"Oh, I'm sorry. It's just that my car is about to run out of gas, and I need to make a phone call to my home girl to meet me at the gas station, so I can get some money. See my phone went dead, and I don't have any change to call her. Your house was the closest without my car stopping." She explained.

"Aiight come in." He stepped back and opened the door a little wider so that the girls could come into the house. He watched as they walked by with tight jean shorts and half shirts on showing off their assets. *Damn*, He thought locking the door behind him.

Tonya was sexy. She was short with a small frame and plump in all the right places. She was light skinned with hazel eyes and a soft-spoken voice like one of the late-night call girls on TV. Caine had always wanted to get with her, but she was too stuck up. She knew how fine she was.

"Where the phone at?" She asked.

"It's over there." Caine responded. He pointed to the direction of the phone then walked back towards the room and sprawled across the bed.

Tonya peeped her head into the back where she could see Caine lying on the bed. She picked up her cell phone and acted as if she was talking to her girlfriend only she was talking to Khalik. "Come in about 10 minutes." She told him. Tonya signaled for Ebony to head towards the back where Caine was while she unlocked the front door. She walked into the room and joined them. Caine lay across the bed on his back watching as Tonya and Ebony began kissing one another. His manhood stood tall, bulging from his boxers.

"Why don't we play a little game?" Tonya said, and she walked over to Caine and began to take his socks off of his feet.

"What game you got in mind?" He asked barely able to speak correctly.

"Let's just say that we are gonna take very good care of you tonight." She took the socks and tied his hands to the bed post really tight then Ebony jumped on the bed climbing on top of him and opened up her shirt. She pulled out her fully developed D cup breast and leaned in over his face. Caine began sucking on her breast like a newborn to a nipple. Tonya pulled down his boxers and climbed on top of him behind her friend. She stroked his manhood with one hand and unbuttoned

Ebony's pants with the other and played with her pussy.

Hassan, Khalik, and the three goons walked into the front door of Caine's house. Hassan whispered for them to check the house for anything they can get some money for and he, and Khalik walked towards the backroom.

"Well, well, well if it isn't that punk motherfucker Caine." Hassan said.

Caine jumped up and looked around Ebony's figure but still saw no one. As he did he ejaculated on his self. "Who the fuck is that?" He squirmed to get up. "Bitch, get the fuck off me."

Tonya and Ebony snickered as they moved to the side and held Caine's arms so that he wouldn't get loose from the socks that tie him to the bed post.

"Fuck is going on, what you niggas doing in my house?" Caine yelled out.

Hassan looked at him in discuss. "I hear you been talking big shit nigga, what's up with that?" He asked.

"What, fuck you talking 'bout. Let me up, so I can bust you niggas ass. You come up in my shit and think you're doing something."

"Jimmy wants to know where his money been going."

"What!"

"The money you be stealing from him, where is it?" Khalik asked.

"I don't know what you're talking 'bout."

"Aiight, well, I'm gone ask you one more time and then that's your ass."

"Where is the money?"

Caine looked around and saw a set up. He didn't care how bad they beat him up; he wasn't giving up the money.

Hassan walked out of the room then stepped back in with the goons. "Maybe this will open your mouth."

The two guys walked over and began beating Caine; one with a chain and the other with a pistol.

"Aiight that's enough" He told them. "You're lucky I'm not gonna have your bitch ass killed for talking all that shit over the phone." He said to Caine. "Aiight y'all we good, take whatever it is you want. This nigga is not going to miss it."

Caine screamed and moaned in agony from the pain. "Ahh."

"Shut the fuck up bitch nigga." Hassan yelled out.

"Tonya, I'm gonna get up with you later, but here you go." He Handed Tonya and Ebony a couple hundred dollars before they exited out the front door.

Caine squirmed around trying to loosen the socks' tide around his wrist to free his self from the bedpost when he finally got one arm unattached. Hassan and Khalik stood there with their backs turned rambling through Caine's drawers when Hassan noticed Caine getting loose. "Oh you're bold huh?"

Caine pulled the sock from his other wrist and started to charge at Hassan when without spoken words and only a split second Hassan and Khalik pulled their guns from the waist of their pants and quickly blew Ciane's chest full of holes. He stopped in his tracks before the force of the bullets sent him crashing down onto the bed. Just as they stopped shooting Khalik noticed a loose floor board that creaked when he took a step forward. He took a step back and bent down. Khalik placed his palm on one side of the wood to allow the other side to lift.

"What is it?" Hassan asked.

Just as Khalik removed the wood piece from the floorboard, he saw stacks of money sitting there. All the money Caine stole from Jimmy and then some. He had been saving more than he was actually spending, and now it was all theirs. Hassan and Khalik gathered up the 50 g's of Jimmy's money that had been missing and placed it in a pillowcase. The remaining 30 g's were placed in another pillowcase to keep for themselves.

They pulled up to the Holiday Inn Hotel, parked the car and got out both were limped over and bruised up, walking into the Hotel. The people stared and whispered with disbelief on their faces as they walked in. They ignored the looks and quietly went upstairs to the room and started to clean themselves up.

"Man I have something in store for those niggas tomorrow." Hassan said pacing back and forth in the small walkway of the room right between the double beds.

"Yeah we need to go back there with some guns or some kind of protection. If this was a plan to get us down here and kill us, we'd be dead. Whatever it is it's fucked up." Khalik stood in the door of the bathroom standing in front of the Hotel mirror looking at his bruised body. What was once a six-pack now looked like a walking corpse that was beginning to rot away slowly from the inside.

"Yeah, well, like I said I got something for their asses so just be down for whatever. We're leaving with that money, but not for Jimmy; he owes us, this one, and I want all 20 thou' of it. This right here is how we come up in the streets." Hassan said continuing to go on talking to Khalik, who had fallen asleep as both lie in the separate beds.

The next morning Khalik woke up looking around, noticing that he was still in the Hotel room. "It's 10:45. Damn! Man, we got to go." He jumped up out of the bed and headed for the bathroom to brush his teeth. "Wake up we got to get that money; it's almost 11:00, get up." Hassan hurried up to get dressed and they stormed out of the front door. They pulled up to the abandoned building and walked in the door.

"I see you finally decided to join us." Bama told them "Show, get them a seat." Big Show shoved them over to the crates that were sitting on the ground. They sat down and started looking around as some of his boys moved in, surrounding them.

"What the fuck is going on?" Hassan said with anger in his voice asking Bama and the rest as they surrounded them.

"Oh, now you want to know what's going on. Well, I'll tell you what's going on. I hear your little young pussy's think you're gonna take over the streets up there in the Chi. Now tell me, how you plan to do this. I can't think of any other way except for you thinking about robbing somebody." Bama's voice became extremely smooth, almost too calm, as he continued to circle around the old wooden crates, chipping of paint, that they had been seated on.

"Nigga, you don't know who talking to or what you're talking 'bout." Hassan told Bama jumping up in his face.

Bama Head butted him, sending him falling to the floor gushing blood from his nose. As Khalik rose up, Big Show grabbed him from behind placing his right arm around his neck; head locking and choking him, barely able to breathe and starting to lose oxygen, Khalik sat still.

"You're fucking with my money when you think about robbing Jimmy. You see the word get around and everybody hears everything, even when you think they're not listening. So, I got a message for you boys, next time I will kill your asses, country style. Now take this 20 g's and get the hell out of town and when you come, come correct and mind your manners when you visit down here in Birmingham." Bama threw the black duffle bag of money to Khalik. "Get the fuck out. Now! He yelled, "'For I change my mind and shoot you niggas."

Big show released Khalik from the headlock; he placed him in, slapping him across the head one last time. He gasped for air, barely breathing. He slowly rose up from the crate he was sitting on; watching to make sure one of them didn't come from behind him swinging or shooting, but they had already gone. Khalik leaned over and helped Hassan up from the ground. "Come on man get up. Don't sweat that shit, we're gonna dead them country motherfuckers."

Khalik leaned back down and unzipped the black duffle bag. It appeared that all the money was there. He could smell the crisp bills as he touched them. *Damn, 20 g's.* He thought as he zipped the bag back up and grabbed it from the ground. "You good man? You need some help walking? Can you see?"

Hassan held his nose. "Yeah man, damn." He said looking at Khalik as if he had just asked a dumb question, with a muffled voice from his hand being covered over his mouth. His nose was gushing blood all down his face, onto his shirt; covering with blood quickly, dripping as they walked out of the abandoned building.

They got into the car. "Here man you want my shirt?" Khalik asked giving him the navy blue Polo shirt that he had on top of his t-shirt to help stop the blood from dripping in the rental car.

"Thanks." Hassan held the shirt in front of his nose to stop the blood from dripping. "Damn! Those niggas busted my shit." Referring to his busted nose.

"Yeah man, look, what happened to the plan you were supposed to have?" Khalik asked sarcastically.

"Khalik, we not at home man we don't know how dirty these country boys can get, but tonight it's all over for 'em."

"What you talking 'bout? What are you thinking?" Khalik asked.

"We scope out Big Show and follow him wherever he goes, then we wait until the area is clear, and we set them motherfuckers on fire." Hassan was enraged with anger, furious from what they had done to him. He felt humiliated in front of Khalik, and he had never wanted him to see him like that again, or anybody else; he was gonna make sure of it.

"Man, hell yeah that's what I'm saying, let's get them, then get back and handle Jimmy's ass."

"We are damn sure not gonna just let 'em get away with this shit?" Hassan said looking at Khalik.

"That's what I'm saying."

"Waiting and watching them could take all day though, so you have got to be prepared to sit and wait, even if it means catching a later flight or driving this motherfucker back ourselves."

"Then we wait for them as long as it takes, even if it's all night. The revenge is on." Khalik appeared down for the plan that was presented to him.

"Then it's on. Let's get these niggas man, shit, cause they either got to pay us or pay the doctor, and we done cashed in on this money so, it's nothing left but to die and it looks like they 'bout to die."

They gave each other a look as if they knew this was the start of what they had been waiting for, power, money, respect, and to be notorious in all of Chicago. These boys were about to come up even if it meant to kill people off, whatever it took had to be done.

Chapter Two

Sweet Revenge

Hassan pulled up down the street in some bushes from the abandoned building; it was getting dark. There they sat for an hour before they saw Bama, Big Show, and the rest of their crew pulling up and going into the building. Hassan and Khalik waited for a minute before they got out of the car and walked through the bushes towards the building, creeping and hiding behind cars to make sure that no one was outside watching out. They had a tank of gasoline and a book of matches that they brought with them.

"Now all we have to do is pour this gasoline around the building, set it on fire, and get the hell out of here." Hassan explained to Khalik as they kept creeping behind the cars.

"Wait, make sure you pour gasoline all over the door. That's the first thing they're gonna try to do is escape." Khalik said to Hassan, reassuring him that they would try to escape once they noticed that the building was on fire.

After creeping and dodging through the cars and bushes, they finally reached the side of the building. Hassan opened the cap to the tank of gasoline catching a whiff into his nose; pouring it all along the sides and bottom of the building. Khalik followed behind him as he finished pouring the gas to watch his back, making sure no one was coming.

"Aiight Khalik, now, light that shit up," Hassan told him, closing the cap on the gasoline tank as he finished pouring the gas down the front of the door, Khalik then lit the fire.

"Run! That shit is spreading fast!" Khalik screamed to Hassan as the flames started to rise like lava flowing from an erupting volcano. They ran away from the building as fast as they could while Hassan was still carrying the tank of gasoline with him, gripping it in his hand, trying not to drop it. They ran back through the bushes and hopped into the rental car.

"Let's go man, drive." Khalik said in a panic.

Hassan started the car. "Wait I got to see if they're gonna make it out of there. If they manage to escape the flames, then we're gonna have to kill them before we leave Birmingham. If we don't they are going to find us and we are as good as dead." They sat back in the car and watched as they ran up out of the building. Khalik and Hassan started to laugh. Just before they all could run out the building exploded; splattering blood and body parts throughout the field.

"Damn! Look at them screaming like some hoes. They're not too tough now are they?" Bama and some of his boys were lying on the ground kicking, screaming, and rolling on the ground covered in flames of fire trying to put their self out with only half of their limbs and body parts still intact.

"Hassan, look man, here come Bama. He looks like he's getting past that shit, he's heading towards us." Bama was the first one to make it out of the building.

He was on the ground crawling towards the cars passing all his boys on the ground either dead or burning to death. Looking at all of their faces as he passed them by, the smell of death covered the atmosphere with burning flesh and gasoline. He cared nothing for them, only saving his self.

Hassan got out of the car taking the gasoline and matches with him. He walked over to Bama and started spreading more gas all over; drowning it in his face.

"No, Wait!" Bama tried pleading for forgiveness, but that didn't matter. He had dealt his hand and played his cards, and lost; now he must pay up and die.

Hassan took one last long hard look into the eyes of the first and only man who would ever make a fool of him again. "Welcome to hell nigga." He set Bama on fire watching him burn, enjoying the vicious smell of flesh in the air.

"Come on man. What the hell are you doing, we go to go." Khalik yelled out the car window.

He jumped into the driver's side of the car and sped off leaving Bama and all his boys dead, sprawled across the ground. They drove back to the Holiday Inn Hotel where they got their bags and headed for the airport.

"Yo, you got the duffle bag man?"

"Yeah I got it." They walked into the airport trying to purchase a ticket leaving from Birmingham to Chicago. "We need a one-way ticket to Chicago ASAP."

The woman at the desk replied. "The next one leaves in about 15 minutes and then there's…"

Hassan quickly interrupted her. "We'll take it." They paid for their tickets and rushed to the terminal where they handed the flight attendant their boarding passes and entered the plane. "Good we made it, now all we need to do is get to Jimmy." Hassan said with treachery in his eyes, looking at Khalik, who knew that they were in for a long ride. They knew that they had to do. What was necessary, even if it meant killing Jimmy to get the respect they deserved and the power they wanted.

Shortly after arriving back in Chicago Khalik and Hassan headed towards Khalik's house contemplating what their next move would be. "Its not going to be easy man, we're talking 'bout one of Chi-towns biggest dealers. He knows just 'bout everybody. I'm down though, he got to pay for this shit one way or the other." No sooner than he finishing his words Khalik's cell phone started to ring. "That's Jimmy." He answered the phone, but before he could get a word out, Jimmy started to yell, sounding as a dissatisfied irate customer.

"Where the fuck have y'all been? It's after 12:00 you were supposed to be here hours ago. I was beginning to think you took off with my money and vanished. Now I know you boys not that stupid are you, trying to pull one over on me." Jimmy said to Khalik over the phone.

"Look, Jimmy......"

Hassan snatched the phone from out of his hand. "Those county ass niggas threatened to kill us right after they kicked our asses."

"Well now, you know you do have a way of getting under the skin. Maybe you shouldn't take things so seriously, I'm sure they were only trying to show you boys how things go down there in Birmingham." Jimmy said sarcastically, laughing.

"You had something to do with that punk ass shit didn't you?" Hassan began to get even angrier at the fact that he knew the answer to the question he was asking and Jimmy seemed to be enjoying the sound of his anger.

"I thought you boys were the real deal. I know Hassan's not going to let some country niggas make him piss his pants like a little bitch. On the other hand, maybe that's what you really are, all bitch. Now come on over here bitch and give daddy his paper." Jimmy insulted him.

The vein in his forehead began to pulsate as the fire in his eyes grew bigger. "Bitch, Nigga I got your Bitch!" Hassan hung up the phone. "We 'bout to go dead this motherfucker," He said pacing through the apartment.

The phone rang again; it was Jimmy calling back. Khalik answered. "Yeah"

"Khalik you and Hassan get this through your heads, if I don't have my money by tomorrow, I'm gonna gut his ass and make you watch. Right after I fuck him like the little bitch that he is then I'm gone kill you." The phone went to a dial tone. Jimmy had hung up.

Khalik heard nothing but silence after that. He knew that they had to Kill Jimmy. Jimmy was known, which meant he knew a lot of people, but there was no way they were going to let him kill them first. They were not going out like bitches.

"Come on Khalik let's go get this nigga. We'll take my car; I already got some shit in the trunk." They walked outside to Hassan's car and opened the trunk.

"Damn, who was you gonna kill?" Khalik asked looking at the amount of ropes, chains, acid, knives, guns, and all kinds of stuff. "Where you get all this from? When did you get this?" He looked around to make sure none of the niggas walking by was paying attention to what was going on.

"That's not important, any ways nobody's gonna mess with us once we get Jimmy's ass out the way. I'm going to make sure they know we are not playing 'round here."

"Hey what up, what y'all doing?" Tre walked outside to the car.

Hassan quickly closed the trunk to make sure he did not see anything. "What's up Tre, we 'bout to make a run, you down?"

"I'm cool."

"Naw, I'm messing with you man I know you're not with that; you and your brother from a different breed. Shit he all nigga and your part something else." Clowning Tre, trying to calm down and show some humor to keep from showing how angry he was in front of him.

"Start the car and let me go holler at Tre for a minute." Khalik took Tre back into the building up to the second floor where they lived.

"I got some serious business to take care of so when I get back home it's gone be late. Make sure you lock the doors and do not answer it for anybody. I will call you before I come so you will know I am coming. Oh, and if anything happens to me and Hassan you make sure you let them crackers know Jimmy Johnson was responsible."

"What's going on Khalik? You sound like you in some trouble or something?" Tre asked as if he could tell from the looks of suspicion on their face what they were about to do.

"Oh naw, I'm just tired that's all, you know, coming straight off the plane with no rest is getting to me a little. Any ways, I'll call you in a little while." Khalik walked out of the front door and headed to the car where Hassan waited.

As they drove off Tre wondered what was really going on. He knew his brother was not telling him everything. *I hope they are not in any trouble with nobody; running from somebody, they owe some money or something.* Tre thought to his self. He knew they could stand their own ground, but he still worried about losing his brother, the only person he had left in his life since their mom died. He would not know what to do if something had happened to him.

Hassan pulled up to Jimmy's house then handed the black leather gloves that he got from out of the trunk to Khalik. He took the two guns from under the driver's seat, placing one in his back pocket, holding the other in his hand; grabbing the duffle bag. It was pitch dark outside.

"Let's go get this nigga." Khalik said.

They rang the doorbell several times. *Oh, I see they came to their senses, otherwise they would have got they asses popped. Youngsters not ready for the shit I can bring in their life.* Jimmy thought, looking at the security monitors in his house.

The guards had left for a short while, so Jimmy was without his protection, but that did not faze him. He answered the door, not re-alizing what was in store for him. "I see you finally decided to show your faces." He said standing in the doorway with a Cuban cigar in his mouth, blowing smoke into their faces, wearing a black silk Versace robe. He pulled the cigar from his lips, ashes falling to the ground. "Now, where is my money?"

Hassan pulled a gun out from his back pocket and put it to Jimmy's head. "Yeah who's the bitch now?" The expression of anger took over his face.

Jimmy's eyes became big as the cigar fell from his fingers; the look of surprise came upon his face. "Oh, so this how its gonna be, huh, young brother; I taught you these streets, and now you're gonna try to rob me of my life and everything I worked hard to build?" Laying the guilt trip on thick

"Shut the fuck up." Khalik said punching Jimmy in the stomach, folding him to the marbled floor in the entrance of the doorway.

"Everything you worked hard to build, fuck you. For two years, we have been busting our ass trying to make you richer, and you get us out there in the country, in the middle of nowhere and try to set us up. Get your ass in the house." Hassan continued to point the gun at Jimmy's head; forcing him into the house. "Khalik, grab the other gun from my back pocket."

Khalik grabbed the gun and began looking around the house when he noticed the security cameras set up in an unused room. He grabbed the tape from the security camera and busted out all the screens, destroying any evidence of them ever being there. Khalik walked back to Hassan and Jimmy, "There's nobody in the house but him." He said.

"Oh, we caught your ass slipping, huh? Khalik, go upstairs and get the stuff out the safe while I keep an eye on his ass. The number to the safe is 7-16-19- 24. The safe is in his office."

"How the hell how did you know 'bout that?" Jimmy said. Khalik looked at Hassan in surprise. He had no idea that Hassan knew as much as he did nor did he realize how well their plan was going.

"You're not too careful with the way you do things Jimmy, you're sloppy. Sloppiness is a bad habit that should be broken." Hassan told him.

Khalik walked in the office and over to the safe, trying to unlock it with the number Hassan had given him. *I hope this shit open.* He thought when a click sound came from the safe as he entered the last digit. *Damn, Hassan, we should have hit this motherfucker sooner.* Khalik started to collect the money from out of the safe, looking around for something to place it in; he noticed a small trashcan with a trash bag lined in it.

He dumped the trash and took the bag out, dropping the money in it and counting the stacks one by one. He collected all the stacks of money and headed back towards the front entrance. "It was 3 million in the safe, but that was it." He said.

"Were you hiding the work?" Hassan asked leading Jimmy into the living room still pointing the gun at his head.

Jimmy slapped the gun away from his head and kneed Hassan in the groin.

"Watch out! Khalik charged at Jimmy's head pistol whipping him and knocking him into the wall.

Hassan folded up a little, while he was still holding on to the gun. He pointed at Jimmy and fired a shot into the wall, then another, purposely missing him both times, so he knew that he was not bull shitting. "Oh, you're trying to play superhero, huh? You just cost yourself a serious ass whoop in' nigga." He grabbed Jimmy by the throat choking him and shoving the gun in his mouth. "Get on your knee's motherfucker." Jimmy slowly kneeled down on the floor gagging on the metal that lay deep in his throat. "Now where is the fucking drugs bitch and don't make me repeat myself again."

Jimmy pleaded with Hassan realizing that he was about to kill him. "Alright man, look, I'll give you whatever you want just put the gun away." He said, barely able to speak with a semi-automatic in his mouth.

"Fuck that where's the stuff at?" Hassan demanded. He looked down at what Jimmy was wearing. "What's that? Is that the black Versace? Take that shit off." Jimmy took the robe off carefully trying not to make any sudden moves with the gun still in his mouth. He reached out, trying to place the silk robe on the floor when Khalik snatched it out of his hand, leaving Jimmy butt naked with his dick hanging. "Little dick motherfucker, Khalik, man put that in the bag. I like that."

"Just shoot this motherfucker and let's go. Kill his ass and let's be out," Impatiently expressing that he was ready to leave since they had already collected the money.

"Where is it?" Hassan said one last time.

"Is there a silent alarm in the house Jimmy?" Khalik asked with anger in his voice, trying to be sure that they covered all of their tracks.

"No." Jimmy was shaken. The tremble in his voice showed through. *Damn, where are these niggas. I'm about to be murdered, and they're out chilling when they supposed to be watching over me and my shit.* He thought.

"Say goodnight." Hassan said pointing the gun back at Jimmy's head about to pull the trigger.

"You niggas not gonna get away with this shit Hassan. My guards will be back in a minute." Jimmy said hoping this would scare them away at the thought of the big black guards with guns. *Fuck! How did I let this go down,* Asking his self?

"Shut the fuck up and bow down bitch."

"Ok wait, the work is in another safe on the wall behind the painting in the living room."

Khalik looked up at Jimmy and gave him an evil glare, then he walked over and removed the painting off the wall where he had seen the safe. "What's the combination?"

"12- 48-5-18" Jimmy said.

Khalik tried the combination number Jimmy gave them. There was a click, and the lock opened. Inside the deep walls of the safe were the work; the heroin and the cocaine. Everything that they had been looking for. "How much is this?" Hassan asked him.

"12 pounds of heroin and about 22 pounds of cocaine, it's all yours take it." Jimmy said nervously.

"Thanks nigga." Hassan looked into Jimmy's eyes, pointing the semi- automatic at him. He wanted to be sure that Jimmy looked directly into the eyes of the young nigga who took it all away. Jimmy stared him back into his eyes hoping that this was not his last breath, staring down the barrel of the gun, when Hassan shot him four times in the head. His brains splattered all over the walls. A puddle of blood covered the marbled floor where Jimmy's head lay and Hassan's face shown spots of red, as well as his clothes. He took the inside of his shirt and wiped the blood from his face, "Let's go Khalik. You got the security tape?"

"Yeah I already took care of that." Khalik was not surprised at all. This was not the first time he had seen Hassan with a gun, and it would not be the last. They grabbed the duffle bag that they brought from the car, placing the work inside. There were several bricks of cocaine. "Damn man we need something else to put this in."

"Yeah you're right we need to get all of this and quick." Hassan said.

"Hold up man." Khalik ran into the kitchen looking into the cabinets for some trash bags. "Here I'll load this up, and you start putting it in the car man." They had about 12 pounds of heroin stuffed in small trash bags. As Khalik finished filling the bags, Hassan loaded them up in the car and the trunk. "I think there's one more bag, the bag with the 30 g's in it. I'll go get it, start the car."

Khalik rushed out the door of Jimmy's house and jumped into Hassan's lime green 87' drop top Chevy as he sped off down the road pulling the top up. This was the beginning for them; the beginning of the come up that they had been waiting for, their chance to finally shine.

It was 2:30 in the morning, and the sirens from the ambulance and police drowned the sound of the wind in the night as they approached the 300,000-dollar home overlooking the Chicago River. The neighbors had heard the shots fired and called the police to check things out.

Detective Beau Whitman, a redneck cop that hated the sight of niggers much less them living in a house bigger than he could afford or in a predominately-white neighborhood, arrived at the scene.

"I heard shots coming from out of the house, and that's when I called the police." The neighbor said nervously not believing this could be going on in the neighborhood that she, and her family had been living in for years. "This type of thing never happens around here. We usually don't even have to lock our doors at night, that's how safe we've always felt."

"Don't worry ma'am we'll take a look and see what all the commotion is about." Detective Whitman assured her as he approached the front door of the house. He walked up noticing that the door was slightly cracked. He pushed the door open.

"Is everyone alright in there? This is the police, if you can hear me let me know your ok." He yelled out hoping to get an answer back. Whitman whispered to his men behind him who were in the position to fire a shot at any given minute. "Cover me, I'm going in." He walked into the house. "Is anyone in here?" As he started to walk further in, he noticed the blood on the floor. "I see blood take cover."

He walked in looking at the blood on the ground and slowly looking up the wall. There he found a black male who seemed to be dead from multiple gunshot wounds to the head. Whitman rushed over to the body to get a pulse already knowing that he was not alive. "Get the coroner over here we got a gunshot victim." The cops hurried to get the coroner on the phone.

"Get those people back in their houses, and I don't want anybody touching anything." *Fucking black ass, I hope you rot in hell you monkey, tainting our good communities with your ghetto women and homeboys drinking 40 ounces and smoking weed.* He thought to his self-wanting to leave the body there and burn the entire house to ashes.

He searched around the house looking for any identification he could find on the dead man when he noticed the picture on the wall, which appeared to have been a safe that was hidden behind it. In the safe was a key, Whitman picked it up and quickly placed it in his pocket when he heard the other cops approaching.

"Any ID on the stiff yet?" He asked the cops that were searching the rest of the house.

"You'll never guess who the stiff is." Detective Whitman replied to his partner, Detective Phil Smith.

"Who?" Smith asked looking as if he cared at all

"Jimmy Johnson." Whitman said.

"The Jimmy Johnson? The Jimmy Johnson who we have been trying to catch for the last few years? The same Jimmy Johnson that was brought up on murder and drug charges and somehow all the evidence got destroyed, that Jimmy Johnson?" He said with a smile on his face as if he had had the pleasure of killing him his self, knowing that he had been the reason for all evidence being destroyed.

"Yeah, well apparently Jimmy wasn't too tough, and he couldn't buy his way out of this one. I always knew his ass would slip up sooner or later, and we have the pleasure of taking him to the morgue." Detective Smith said smiling devilishly. "Shit this is the best news I've had all week." He said as they walked out of the house.

"Yeah, check out what I found in the safe." He pulled the key out of his pocket and handed it to Smith. "My guess is that it goes to a safety deposit box.

"And where there is a safety deposit box, there is usually a treasure of goods behind it." Smith replied.

"Hey what's going on? We have the right to know for our safety." The neighbor woman asked interrupting the detectives in their mischievous conversation.

"For your safety you better lock your doors because the niggers are on the loose." Whitman replied to her as she looked with disbelief of what was just said. He walked toward his car yelling out to the cops surrounding the area. "I need this area taped we have a homicide on our hands." He got the chief of police on the phone. "Yeah chief we got a homicide on the call over in The Gold Coast. Black male with multiple gunshot wounds to the head."

"Be sure everything is airtight, and I don't want any of our guy's fingerprints all over the place destroying any evidence. Do we know who he is?" The chief of police asked Whitman.

"Drug lord Jimmy Johnson."

"Uh huh, I see somebody finally stopped him. Well, keep me updated on things. I want to know everything." Chief hung up the phone.

Fat bastard, He thought.

A red Mercedes pulled up creeping towards Jimmy's house passing on by not trying to be noticed. "The laws are all over the place man. What happened?" Jimmy's guard Rick said, speaking to another guard of Jimmy's, Chad.

"Oh, they got the place taped off. Damn, I wonder if Jimmy's still there."

"You don't think.... naw, hell naw not Jimmy."

"Damn nigga I told you we should have come right back man. What the fuck we gonna do?" Chad said growing nervous by the minute.

"Let's get the hell out of here and call Jimmy." Rick picked up the cell phone and called Jimmy's cell. The phone went to the voicemail on the first ring. "Damn he's not answering his phone."

"You know he turns that shit off at a certain time, unless he's expecting somebody to call him."

"Fuck it man let's go; I can't afford to get caught up in nothing else. I'm not trying to go to jail, fuck that, I'm on papers." Rick said driving off.

"Detective's Whitman and Smith I want to see you in my office." The chief announced heading back into the office. They walked in and sat down closing the door behind them. "What do we have on the Johnson case?"

"We don't have any new information yet chief. Everything seems to be leading us into a dead end." Whitman tried explaining to the chief. "Were doing the best we can besides, he's better off now that he's dead."

"I'm gonna forget that I just heard that little remark. You are here to do a job not give your personal opinion on what is good for someone. I want the two of you to bring me some new leads and evidence concerning this case. I'm giving you one week, otherwise I'm going to assign somebody who can handle it."

"We'll get on it chief as soon as possible." Smith said kissing the chief's ass trying to suck up. They walked out of the office and out of the precinct. "Who the fuck cares about this nigger, I mean that's just one less drug dealer we have to worry about polluting our streets and neighborhoods with their drugs, and gang bangs." He fired up a cigarette.

"They're not going to find out that we had something to do with those niggers that killed him. All we need to do is find someone to pin it on, and case closed." Whitman told Smith.

"No one knows about that but us three. Besides, it's not like we killed him. I don't think he would do something so stupid as to mention us."

"Yeah well who knows who he's told, he's too cocky."

"I admit he isn't the smartest, but he isn't that stupid." Smith flicked the cigarette butt on the ground. "For all the chief and the rest of the department know the people who killed Jimmy could have easily just been trying to rob him. They don't know if this was a premeditated murder, and we have that key that no one knows about except for us."

"Smith we got to take care of this nigga or we're gonna be the ones in that jail cell for life." "Whitman walked back into the precinct building.

We just need to keep a close eye on things to make sure we are cleared or like he said get rid of them. Smith thought.

The phone began to ring. *Damn who is this calling me?* She turned over to look at the clock sitting on the nightstand by the bed. *It's 5:00 in the morning.* She answered the phone. "Hello"

"Yes is there a Janae Luvell available?"

"This is she, who is this?" Lovely asked wondering who this man was who felt the need to call her house this early in the morning.

"This is homicide Detective Phil Smith of the CPD calling about your uncle Jimmy Johnson."

"Homicide, wait a minute. What is going on? Is my uncle alright?" Lovely started to panic. She jumped up out of the bed and turned on the table lamp.

"Yeah we believe your uncle was a victim of foul play. We know that he was one of the biggest dealers in Chicago so obviously there's going to be a lot of suspected persons of interest."

"Foul play, Homicide, what…No, oh my god what is going on."

"Well your uncle was shot in the head several times in his house and there was a safe that appeared to have been emptied along with the tapes to the security cameras that were busted."

Lovely let out a loud horrible scream, "Oh god no, why is this happening? Not my uncle Jimmy. Who did this?"

"We don't know but we do know that it was drug related, and the neighbors say they saw two black males driving off but there was no clear description of the car or them except that they were younger. We're going to need you to come down and take care of some things."

"You said there were reports of two young black males." As she wiped her eyes, trying to calm herself down she silenced waiting to hear his answer again hoping that she heard him wrong.

"Yeah, but that's all we've got. The sooner you can come out the quicker we can get a little more information about your uncle. Contact me as soon as you land in town."

Lovely hung up the phone dazing into the glare from the light hitting her eyes. She could not believe what she was hearing about her uncle, the only family left in her life now gone by some young punks who did not have the balls to go out there and make their own money, so they had to take her uncle's. She knew that she had to find the person who did this. *Prejudice ass police down there not going to do anything. I'm gonna have to do this on my own.* The tears flowed down her face like a waterfall filling her eyes more and more as the thought of her uncle's murder played repeatedly in her mind. *Whoever did this is going to pay.*

As the night crept, the tears began to moisten her pillow like a dampened cloth. Lovely cried all night. Confused and distraught about what has happened to her uncle and why anyone would want to do this to him. She had to go home. She had not been there in a while, and even though she lived in the same state, she just had not had the time to go back, nor did she want to, until now.

Early into the morning lovely picked up the phone and called the only person who she could count on for anything besides her uncle, her best friend Nyla.

As the phone began to ring on the other end, Nyla answered, "Hello"

"Hi, it's me. I'm sorry to bother you so early, but I needed to talk to someone."

"Oh my God, Love are you alright? I heard about your uncle; I am so sorry. If there is anything that I can do for you just let me know"

"Yeah, thank you so much for the support. I don't know what I'm gonna do." Lovely told Nyla "I still can't believe he's gone."

"Maybe you should come down and stay for a while and get your mind off of things."

"Yeah, I think your right, besides, I have to come and take care of all the funeral arrangements."

"Well, just keep your head up. Everything is going to be all right. I will help you through this." Nyla assured her.

"Thanks, I don't know what I would do without you. Any ways I have a few things to wrap up here, so I will be calling you in a few days when I get there."

"O.k. if you need to call me anytime day or night, you know I am always here for you."

"Thank you Nyla, really."

"Listen to me. Whatever you have to do, I am down with you, just call me. I love you, and I will talk to you soon." They both said their goodbye's and hung up the phone. The last words that Nyla had spoken stuck into Lovely's mind. She had to think of a way to get whoever did this back, but first she had to find out who did this, and she would soon.

Nyla hung up the phone and turned over in the bed, facing Khalik as he lay there awakening from his sleep.

Chapter Three

The Setup

"Hey what up, what's going on?" Darrell stopped, talking to Khalik and Hassan as they stood on the block.

"What up D what you doing 'round here man?" Hassan asked.

"Y'all didn't hear? Word on the streets is somebody that was working for Jimmy is the ones who popped him. Be careful man these crackers looking for anybody."

"Naw man it's still hard to believe that he was killed. I mean Jimmy knew a lot of people so it could have been anybody out to get him."

"Yeah, Hassan is right man you know shit is funny like that around here, there's no telling who popped him." Khalik added.

"Yeah well I was 'round the way, and I thought I would give you boys the heads up. So, y'all good on everything?"

"Yeah you know us, we good."

"Alright then holler at me if you need me," Darrell drove off.

"Fuck!" Khalik blurted out, pacing back and forth.

"Don't sweat that shit man they don't have any evidence. We got everything, in order so we're good."

"Yeah I hope you're right nigga. What about the gun that was used, it can't be traced can it?"

"Hell naw, w set I told you. There isn't any going to tie us to this, we good man, relax."

"Yeah, fuck it, you're right."

"Damn right I'm right Khalik, chill." Hassan knew the police could not connect them to the murder, and even if they did have a little evidence it would never stand up in court, but they didn't; they had nothing to go off, and the case was a dead end. Even though he did not show it, he was a little worried about Khalik finding out about the deal he had made with Detective's Whitman and Smith.

As Hassan stood there, he thought about the way Jimmy was killed and how killing him had been a set up way before he, and Khalik went to Birmingham. How those two crooked cops had approached him before any of that other stuff with Jimmy went down.

Damn, this is crazy; he thought to his self, *oh well what is done is done, fuck that hoe ass nigga.*

We have been trying to get Johnson for years now and still nothing. There has got to be a slip up somewhere, and when there is we're going to be right there to catch his ass." Whitman told Smith as they strolled up through the Cedar Park Projects.

"Speaking of slip up, there goes one of his little runners right there, Hassan." Smith pulled up alongside the street where Hassan was standing on the corner.

"Man, fuck, here come these cracker ass laws." He said aloud to his self, turning his back and dropping the bag of crack from his pocket into the dirt covering it with his foot.

"Well, well, well long time no see Hassan, or what is it you go by these days?" Smith gave a suspicious smirk. "What have we been up to?"

"Man I'm just standing here minding my own business; y'all can't fuck with me about shit, I'm clean."

"Is that why you thought you could hide this bag of dope in the dirt?" Whitman pulled the bag up from out of the dirt and held it up in Hassan's face. "Does this look like dope to you boy?"

"That shit is not mine. Y'all put that there." Hassan said as he looked off, started to become nervous knowing that the two officers where shady and prejudice. They would go to any length to see a black man locked up or dead.

"You wouldn't be lying to us boy now would you?" Smith leaned into Hassan and whispered in his ear with the smell of coffee and cigarettes on his breath.

"How about you come and take a ride with me, and Smith here and let us buy you a beer, so we can have a little talk with you."

"Hell naw, I can buy my own beer, besides y'all can't arrest me. I haven't done anything. What the hell y'all want to talk to me for anyway?"

"Why don't you just come with us and find out." Whitman grabbed his arm.

"I'm not going nowhere with you crackers, get the fuck off me," Snatching his arm back away from Whitman.

"You're gonna come with us or your black ass is going to jail. I'm sure they would love to get their hands on a sweet piece of dark meat like you," Smith warned him of the consequences if he did not come with them.

"Now get your ass in the car and there won't be any trouble." Whitman opened the back door to the car.

"Damn, look can I just meet y'all somewhere?" Hassan asked trying to persuade his way out.

"Oh what's the matter you scared Jimmy's going to find out that you have been talking to the cops? If it makes you feel any better we'll handcuff you, huh, how about that?" Whitman pulled out the cuffs and put them on Hassan's hands placing him into the back seat of the police car. As the police car drove off there stood a man smoking on a cigarette as he came from around the building by the corner where Hassan was talking to the two police officers.

They drove to a nearby dead-end street by a construction site where there was nothing but field, grass, and dirt.

"Where we at, this doesn't look like any bar, what the fuck is going on? You crackers gonna try to kill me?"

Smith pulled Hassan out of the back seat "Shut the fuck up!" He punched him in the stomach. "Fucking black ass punk, don't know when to shut up."

Hassan leaned over in pain from the blow to his stomach, but it did not faze him too bad. "What you want with me?" He asked looking up at the both of them.

"We have a proposition for you. We know you work for Jimmy on the streets; you and your friend Khalik is his best runners. We want you to take him out."

"What! You want me to kill him, man look, find somebody else to do your dirty work," Hassan said trying to stand his ground.

"Well we can just go ahead and bust your ass for possession right now." Smith reminded him.

"Why you want me to do this shit? Why can't you get somebody else to get rid of him?"

"We know you know a little about how he operates, his security, and were he falls weak at. Who better to do it than somebody that works for him, somebody that can get close to him? Nobody can do this job better than you can. We know that in the streets, you and Khalik are feared and respected more than some of his other runners."

"Ok so suppose I do help y'all then what's in it for me?" Hassan said treating it as if he was a professional businessman.

"Well, me and Smith here will make it worth your wild. We will give you all the stuff you need to get rid of him and let you keep whatever it is that you want from his house, including the money and the dope."

"How am I supposed to believe that, you mean to tell me if I find any dope or money, I can keep it, and I won't get my crib busted in the next day with a warrant for my arrest for murder and possession?"

"Yeah that's what we're saying. You do this, and we won't fuck with you." Smith confirmed his questions.

"Why y'all won't just bust him the way normal cops do? I mean, why you want him killed so bad?"

"Well he killed a really good friend of mines on the force years ago it was my partner, someone I considered as my brother during a bust. He lost his life while I just got a graze to the shoulder, and Jimmy got away. So, you see this shit is personal, now are you in or do we have to take you down to the station." Smith looked at Hassan with anger and revenge in his eyes as he lied to him to gain a bit of trust and respect, a look that Hassan knew all too well.

Hassan thought about it and he sometimes hated Jimmy, but he was not sure if he wanted to kill him. "Give me a few days to figure out some things, like how I'm going to get rid of him."

"Alright you got three days, but in the meantime we got you some stuff to help you get the job done. Meet us back here tonight at midnight and make sure you come by yourself." Whitman told him taking off the handcuffs.

Smith and Whitman got back into the car and drove off leaving Hassan standing in the dead-end road. "So y'all just gonna leave me out here!" He yelled to them as the car drove off down the rocky road.

"Catch a cab back you can afford it." Whitman yelled out the window looking at how pitiful Hassan looked. They laughed, "Now all we have to do is sit back and watch this nigger do our dirty work."

"No blood on our hands." Smith replied.

"Yeah well technically we could be put away for a long time for this so I just hope that we can trust him to keep his mouth shut otherwise we're going to have to get rid of him, ourselves and his little friend."

Less than a week after her uncle's murder lovely walked into Jimmy's house removing the yellow tape from the entrance of the door. As she began to walk towards the picture in the front room, she noticed a plaque that was her uncle's favorite, it wrote: "*Believe, You Shall Not, In the Eyes Blinded By Deception.*" And the plaque was quoted with Jimmy Johnson written at the bottom. She picked up the plaque and placed it into her purse, then quickly ran into the front room to the hidden safe behind the picture where she searched inside for the key, but could not find it. Lovely could not find anything. She knew her uncle told her if anything happened to him that the key would be there, but it was gone. Who would take a key, unless they somehow had known about the safety deposit box?

Lovely was confused and angry at the same time she looked up and started to walk around the crime scene. The splatter of blood and brains covered the walls as if someone was trying for a new paint color, reeking with an odor of death in the air. The sight of the crime scene made her sick to her stomach. She wanted to hold it in, but before she could cover her mouth, she vomited, feeling as if she was choking, she could not breathe. Lovely ran out of the house quickly, gasping for air as she tried catching her breath.

The police had not contacted her since they told her about the murder. She finally caught her breath and rushed to the car driving like a bat out of hell to the precinct. Lovely walked in, "Where the hell is Detective Smith?"

"Excuse me ma'am I'm gonna need you to calm down and tell me what can I do for you?" The officer at the front desk replied as she continued to act hysterically. "Ma'am if you don't calm down I'm going to have to show you to the door, otherwise you'll be spending a few hours in one of those cells."

"Yeah I'm Detective Smith, who are you?"

"My name is Janae Luvell you contacted me about the murder of my uncle Jimmy Johnson a few days ago. I just got in town, and I have been to the house and seen the shit splattered all over the walls. What the hell is going on? Why aren't you doing your damn job?" She yelled in Smith's face, "If you bastards aren't going to do something, then I will." Lovely started to walk off like a mad woman as almost everyone in the precinct's eyes was on her.

Smith ran behind her outside, "Hey, hey wait a minute." Lovely turned around with tears in her eyes. "I'm doing whatever I can to find out who did this, but we need more time on this." As much as he could not stand the site of anything darker than the light shade of dirty-blond hair on his head, he admired the beauty of her face. Smith put his hand on her shoulder. "Look, why don't me and my partner meet you at the coffee shop down the street in about a half an hour, and you let me buy you a cup of coffee, so we can discuss your uncle's case."

She looked at him with the tears still watering up her eyes. "30 minutes, and don't be late." Walking off as if he had no choice but to do what she says.

He stared at her walking away. *Damn, I have never seen a more beautiful black bitch in my life. She cannot be a fucking nigger, there is no way in hell look at that long hair and those grey eyes.* Smith thought to himself not believing the feeling he felt. His dick was getting hard just looking at her. He knew he had to snap out of it. *What am I thinking? Of course, she is.* He thought, walking back into the precinct adjusting from the semi hard on bulging through his pants.

There across the street sat a black Lexus with dark tinted windows that were slightly rolled down and was parked directly across from the precinct, as the person in it sat and watched every move both detectives, Smith and Lovely had made, Smith was unaware of the car.

Lovely arrived at the coffee shop 10 minutes early before Detective's Smith and Whitman. The waitress came to the table. "What can I get for you?" She said with a little quirkiness.

"Yes, let me get a Hazelnut Latte with an extra shot of Espresso, low-fat milk, and double up on the whipped cream with just a hint of nutmeg on top." *Hell, I'm going to need something strong for this. I wish I had some Hennessy.* She thought, not caring about the added on calories.

"Alright is that all?"

"Yes"

"I'll be back with your order shortly just holler at me if you need anything else." The waitress walked off.

Lovely made a phone call. "Yeah it might be a little longer so just sit tight. I'm meeting with...."

"Mrs. Luvell this is my partner Whitman." Smith said sneaking up behind her startling her.

"I have got to go." Lovely quickly hung up the phone. "Hi" Shaking Whitman's hand.

The Detectives sat down as the waitress walked over to hand lovely her Latte. They placed an order for two black coffees. "I wanted to talk to you here because we have a bit of information about your uncle's murder. We believe the two young men that murdered him worked for him. Hassan and Khalik, two of his top runners were seen leaving his house and word on the streets is that they are the ones who did it."

"What!" Lovely was confused. *Why would they do something like this? I guess this was some type of setup or something all along. She* thought. "So you think they set him up?"

"Well we know that there were some drugs in a safe he had in the living room hidden behind a large picture framed art. We found traces of residue in the safe, so we know that they got that and possibly some money." Whitman explained.

"This is confidential and we want to help you put these two ass holes under the jail where they belong. The only problem is will you be willing to go along with the plan?" Smith asked her.

"My uncle was murdered and I'm gonna do anything to help put these motherfuckers out of their misery." Lovely looked at Smith as if she knew this was illegal, but she did not give a damn.

Everything her uncle had was hers and whatever they took, they were taking away from her. *Khalik and Hassan, why did they do it? Which one pulled the trigger and how could they have had the chance to kill him,* Lovely thought to herself. She knew that her uncle was well known and, many people were jealous of him and for that, they wanted him dead, but she wondered which one of them could have been the brains behind it all or did they have some help.

12:00 midnight and pitch dark outside, Hassan waited for the Detectives to meet him at the same construction site, they took him to three days earlier. They pulled up next to Hassan's car as they all got out. "Alright so where's the stuff?"

"Before we go on any further are we already clear on what the deal is?" Whitman asked.

"Yeah man."

"Good then, don't mess this up boy, or we gonna have your ass lying in the morgue and I will personally put you there myself."

"Whatever, man just give me the stuff so I can go." Hassan told him. They walked over to the unmarked police car that the Detectives were in, and Smith opened the trunk. "Damn, what the hell y'all want me to do? Kill him or execute his ass?" Hassan could not believe what he saw. Even though he knew they were some crooked ass cops seeing, it in his face was realistic.

"Look, it doesn't matter what you use and how you use it just make sure the black motherfucker is dead and make it look good, professional, no sloppiness, or we can't save your ass." Smith told him.

"I know what I'm doing just make sure you hold up your side, or I'm gonna have y'all cracker asses in jail with my black ass, only I'm not going to be the one keeping the inmate off me." Hassan grabbed the stuff and loaded it into his car.

Whitman stopped him as they were about to drive off. "You just remember this is between the three of us, and nobody else knows about this, not even your buddy Khalik, not unless you want to see his little brother hanging from a tree with his dick in his mouth." They both began to laugh. "Oh yeah, when the job is done you make sure you give us a call." Smith said, throwing his card out of the window at Hassan's feet as they sped off.

Sick motherfucker, Hassan thought. He knew that there was no way that Khalik could find out about this or Tre would be the one paying and him, and Khalik would be going away for the rest of their life. They were the only family he knew, and he would protect them as he would his very own self even if it meant to kill for them. He sat in the driver's seat of his car daydreaming about the first time he had met Khalik.

It was back at the age of 13 when Khalik just moved down from Jersey where he, and his brother was staying with his father who was sentenced in East Jersey State Prison for life for murdering two guys who owed him some money for some dope, he fronted them. The game was in his blood, and it was only a matter of time before he discovered his true street hustle.

Late night Cabrini-Green and the atmosphere graced with busted crack pipes and broken bottles, the sound of hustlers in the air at 2:00 in the morning. Khalik awoke to the sound of ruckus coming from the walls of his bedroom. He rose up from the twin-sized bed where he lay and walked into the front of the small two-bedroom apartment. Khalik continued to hear the sounds of curse words and banging as he peeped his head outside of the front door. He stepped out into the hall watching as the front door of the apartment next to theirs was cracked. Khalik could see the boy being slammed onto the ground as the man stomped and kicked him in the head. He leaned in to take a closer look when the door creaked.

The man looked over at Khalik, "What the fuck, oh you must want some too, huh?" Khalik turned as he tried to hurry back into his apartment but was grabbed by the arm. "Get your ass in here. So you like looking in on other folk's business. I'll show your little punk ass." The man grabbed the belt off from the chair and raised his arm into the air about to strike Khalik with the buckle from the belt.

Khalik was scared even though his father was in the drug life, he and his brother were never around this type of thing. Their father made sure that they were taken care of and was not exposed to the life that he had become accustomed to growing up in East Jersey. "I'm sorry, please don't hit me," as he raised his arms to protect his face from the force of the buckle. A boom sound traveled through the dirty beige carpet as the man dropped to the floor. Khalik rose up moving his hands from in front of his face. The man was laying there knocked out cold.

"You ok man?" Hassan stood over him asking, "Let me help you up." Hassan helped Khalik up from off of the floor.

"Why was he hitting on you like that? Who is that man?"

Hassan looked at Khalik as the blood from his head ran down his face passing the black and blue eye dripping onto his shirt. "That's my dad."

Hassan's dad started moaning as he began to wake up from the sleep that the liquor bottle that was busted across his head sent him into. Hassan ran into the kitchen, grabbed his dad's gun from a shoebox on top of the icebox, and ran back into the living room. Khalik looked into Hassan's eyes, all he could see was the anger and revenge. He knew that whatever took place at that very point this was something he could never speak of again nor could he ever tell anyone. Hassan stood over his dad with the 48-caliber gun, with the silencer on it, pointed to his head.

"You little black bastard, I wish you were never born. Go ahead, do it, shoot me. Your sorry ass doesn't even have the guts, you're just like your bitch of a mother." Hassan's dad said slurring his words.

A silent pop sounded as he fired a shot into his dads head. The splatter of blood covered the floor dripping along the black leather chair in the living room with a puddle seeping from the back of his head. Hassan looked, as the blood puddle grew larger. He had become obsessed with the immediate power he had from the gun. Hassan fired once more into his dad's chest, splattering the heartless bastard whom he had known to be dad but was really a drunken monster.

"Who's the black bastard now bitch ass nigga?" Hassan was fearless he knew that at this moment in time he could never be afraid of anything or anyone. Not at any time would he let another human being treat him as if he was a piece of crap. This was the beginning, as they both knew it and a form of a lifelong friendship and brotherhood.

Chapter Four

The Funeral

The wake was filled with hustlers and dope boys. Women were crying and falling along the floor screaming and hollering. As the service began and the preacher spoke the words from the Bible, Lovely looked around the room to acknowledge every face that appeared. The atmosphere was merely the vision of a poorly written fictitious horror movie. The women were making fools of themselves and overacting. The cries were only from the loss of all the lavish gifts and money not of Jimmy's death.

The other hustlers appeared distant and impatient. They walked in with their overpriced suits and women on their sides as if it was their duty to pay their respects to the man who left a piece of the streets. Nevertheless, they made it their business to make sure his death was real. His runners stood along the walls in the back of the church as if they were on the street corner waiting on a drug deal. The entire room was a joke.

Lovely thought she had seen it all until she noticed two guys sitting in the front row as she continued to walk. She reached the bench and sat down. She could feel the eyes of the room wondering who she was. Her head was covered with a long silken black scarf, and dark sunglasses to cover her face. She wore a fitted black ensemble with just enough room in it to show her figure.

Halfway through the service Nyla walked in with a sway in her hips towards the front row with all eyes on her. The guys drooled with their eyes, and the women curled up their noses at the unknown beauty. She sat down next to Lovely. "I'm sorry I'm late but there was an accident, and traffic was backed up." Nyla whispered.

"It's alright as long as you made it." Lovely responded back.

Nyla looked up and noticed Khalik and Hassan at the other end of the front row. Khalik winked his eye, and she cracked a smile. Lovely sat next to her with her head down praying to God as she thought about her uncle's death. Right away, she noticed Khalik and Hassan, but they were unaware of her. *They sit and come to his funeral after setting him up for death. The nerves they have.*

The preacher spoke, "Let us bow our heads and pray."

Lovely walked up to the casket and kneeled down in front to bow her head and pray. The entire church was silent except for the sound of the preacher. She opened her eyes looking around the church room then grabbed the pocketknife that sat in her clutch. As the preacher continued she rose up from the floor, bent down, and kissed the closed casket. Then she whispered "God forgive me." Lovely walked over to Khalik and Hassan and stopped in front of them. She pressed the release to let out the blade on the pocketknife.

"In Jesus' name, Amen." The preacher finished.

Just as everyone opened their eyes, the splatter of blood covered lovely's face as she sliced their throats all in one swing. The church was filled with screams.

"Hallelujah and praise Jesus." The preacher shouted out and Lovely opened her eyes. Her thoughts had been so clear that she would have sworn it was real. She wanted them dead, and she would do anything to get her uncle back. However, that would never be. Therefore, the only thing to do was to avenge his death and her broken heart.

The funeral finally ended, and everyone began to exit through the church doors after. Khalik and Hassan stood close to the exit and thanked everyone for coming out.

Khalik looked up at the casket ad noticed Nyla standing there with the unknown beauty in black. "Man, check this out. I'm not the smartest motherfucker but I know she doesn't think we don't realize who she is."

"Who are you talking 'bout?" Hassan asked.

"I'm talking 'bout the bitch in black looking like the grim reaper and shit. That's lovely man. She just dressed up and disguised."

Hassan squinted his eyes a little and took a harder look. "Oh yeah, that's her."

"Yeah, well its nothing. She doesn't know anything so why worry. If she wants to play that little game, then so be it. As long as she stays in her lane, she's good."

Lovely bent down and began to pray in front of the casket. She thought about the vision she had of slicing their throats and killing them, but that would be too easy. She had to get them slow and painful in the worst way, and she knew exactly how to do it.

Chapter Five

The Beginning

Lovely still could not believe that her uncle was gone. The only family that she had now was Nyla, who had decided to move closer to where her uncle Jimmy stayed for a few months, just so they could think about opening another business. Lovely was heartbroken, she thought about the last conversation she had with her uncle.

"Hey baby girl how's it going?" Jimmy asked his Niece Janae.

"Oh good, I'm fine." She replied.

"How's the business doing? I hear it's making more money."

"The business is doing good Uncle Jimmy you know how it is out here."

"Yeah, well I called to see if my favorite, lovely, niece needed anything, or if you thought about coming out here to see me. You know it has been a long time since I had seen your face. I'm not getting any younger." He said to her sarcastically, laughing.

"Alright, I guess you're right; I will check on that." She said. "So how are you? You sound a little stressed, is everything alright out there?"

"Yeah, I'm alright just fucking with them two youngsters I got running for me; the young Chi-town boys are what I call them, Khalik and Hassan. I believe you met them briefly before. Youngsters, reminds me all too well about when I was young. But, enough about my business, I have a little something for you." Jimmy said.

"Well what is it? You know you don't have to keep buying and sending me stuff; I can take care of myself." Lovely insisted.

Well, since I never had any kids of my own then I have to spoil my only niece. Now I need you to listen to me carefully. There is a large sum of money that I put away especially for you. I have a safety deposit box that I have placed your name on as a co-authorizer just you and me are able to have access to the box. I have the key here with me in the safe, and you are the only one who knows about it. If anything were to happen to me, then everything in that box goes to you." Jimmy explained.

"What do you mean if anything ever happens to you?" She asked, "Why you talking like that? Did something happen?" She continued to question.

"No, no, I don't want you to worry about it. I just like to plan ahead so if I were to get sick or anything, then you would be taken care of. I do not want you to ever have to worry about anything. Any ways, I have some business to take care of so why don't you call and let me know when you're gonna come on down to see me."

"Um, Uncle Jimmy, before you go, did I hear you say Khalik and Hassan?" She asked. "Why you still got them around?"

"Yeah, I know; they are a bit reckless, but you know the game. Shit, I don't know who the hell else in these streets gonna be putting up with them." *Their Lucky I don't put their ass to rest.* He thought to his self. "Any ways baby girl, I got some business to take care of so, I love you, and I will talk to you soon."

"Love you, bye." Lovely Hung up the phone, *Uncle Jimmy doesn't sound like everything is all right. Maybe it is time I go down there and see him; I know it has been a while, and we do stay in the same state.* Thinking to herself as she stared into the mid air. Her mind was boggled. She could not help but to think about him mentioning Khalik and Hassan, and the thought of them still working for her uncle all of this time; it sickened her. She remembered when they first met, way before her uncle had introduced them, something her uncle Jimmy was well unaware of. Lovely thought back to the sweet, sensitive, and very persistent Khalik, who was nothing like the street person that most everyone else knew him as.

Summertime, Lovely sit out on the balcony of the luxury apartment sweating and trying to enjoy the weather as the drips of sweat began to roll down her brow. She took a sip of the Hennessy on the rocks from her luxury cognac glass from Italian crystal, hand-made and decorated with pure gold, wiping her forehead. "Damn Nyla It's hot out here." She complained to her best friend as they both began sweating from drinking the cognac in the scorching sun, appearing hotter than it actually was.

Lovely and Nyla had been friends for about four years where they met in the shopping area of The Magnificent Mile in Givenchy, racing to buy the last of a pale pink spaghetti strap dress draped in lace. After realizing that neither of the curvy beauties could fit in a size four they continued to laugh and joke as they shared coffee at a nearby restaurant admiring, the thousands of blooming tulips that grace The Magnificent Mile. From that moment on the two were inseparable and became roommates shortly thereafter. Together they owned a spa business on Michigan Avenue of Chicago where they serviced their clientele with an all out house of grooming. The spa offered over 10 different therapeutic body massages, facials, tanning, mud baths, a fitness center, and an attached hair salon and nail shop.

"Shit, tell me about it. I'm so hot I feel like I just peed on myself." Nyla began to open her legs, hoping a breeze of air would come through the striped Victoria Secret loungewear shorts. "I'll be back girl; I think I need to go wash up and change my panties," Noticing that her laced underwear was suddenly drenched in sweat. Nyla was just as beautiful and graceful in appearance as Lovely, but with a somewhat nasty and ghetto attitude.

Lovely walked down to take Nyla's teacup Yorkshire terrier puppy to relieve herself. She walked along the sidewalk outlining the newly placed grass near the large tree in the front entrance area by the security gate. As the yorkie continued to sniff, lovely noticed a 1997 White BMW 528i with cream leather interior, and the windows rolled down playing Notorious Big's Mo Money, Mo Problems. The car stopped pulling alongside of her.

"What's up, I see you're admiring the ride you want to hop in and go for a spin wit' me?" Khalik told her speaking over his friend in the passenger's side with confidence that he was all of that and then some.

"Please, I mean your ride is right but it sure isn't anything I can't afford myself." She replied back thinking of her 1997 Blue Ashton Martin DB7 with cream leather interior that her uncle had just purchased for her.

"Aiight then, I feel that Well, since you can afford your own that means you're up on my level already so why don't we get together and have dinner or something." Khalik showed his pearly white smile glowing with his succulent lips as he spoke. "You know, since we both can afford our own and all."

Lovely chuckled, "O.k. I guess I was a little snotty just then. So I guess we even on that."

"So, can I get your number and call you sometime or what?" He insisted.

She paused for a second, then thought. *I don't know Love he sounds a little street, but he is riding big, and he does look fine. Shit, I need some on-call dick in my life right now any ways, so what the hell.* "Alright," She wrote the number down on a piece of paper he handed her.

"What's up? You got a friend who looks as good as you do." Hassan asked, eyeballing her.

"I don't know; we'll see." She said turning her eyes back towards Khalik as she gave Hassan attitude because he was sitting in the passengers' side.

"Aiight, well I'll give you a holler." Khalik and Hassan drove off turning up the music as they exited the complex.

Damn he was fine. Wait until I tell Nyla this, oh that bitch is gonna be so jealous, Lovely thought to herself as she could picture the jealousy on Nyla's face. "Chanel, come on girl lets go. She called for the yorkie to come." Lovely walked back towards the apartment building, stopping at the front door to key in the code to let her in then walked up and into the apartment.

"Uh uh, who was that in that BM' girl?" Nyla asked rushing towards the door before she could even get in good.

"Ooh, you are so nosey." Knowing that her friend had been watching out from the balcony since you could overlook the entire area from their apartment. They were not too far up from the ground. "His name is Khalik and yes he was in a BM' so you know he up on my status girl."

"Yeah, you need to find out if he got a friend." Nyla rolled her head as if she wanted to tell her she needed to peep game for her friend cause that's what friends do.

"Well he has a friend, but of course, he was riding in the passenger side." Lovely said as if he was broke.

"Shit if he's riding in a BMW I know the nigga friend got to be riding in something just as nice if not better. What did he look like cause if he fine then it is worth looking into? Shit if he's ugly it's worth looking into." *You can never have too much money*. She thought to herself.

"Uh uh, you ought to be a shame of yourself. Well, I guess hoes need money too." Lovely said throwing the pillow from the couch at her face laughing at her own joke.

"Whatever, you just a hater," She said embracing her gold-digging talents, although she needed no man for nothing, it did not bother her to spend somebody else's money. "Any ways, all I'm saying is, find out what his friend is all about because I do need me a new play toy."

"Uh huh" Lovely looked at Nyla and grinned as she walked off into the bedroom.

A week later and still nothing from Khalik, Lovely almost forgot about even meeting him. Getting off work on a Friday evening, she and Nyla walked into their luxurious apartment.

"Oh girl my feet are killing me." Nyla said kicking off a pair of three-inch butternut Manolo Blahniks to match her cream, silk chiffon dress with a butternut Pashmina as she plumped down onto the sofa. "I need me a glass of Hennessy or wine; you want some?" She asked Lovely.

"Yes, you read my mind."

"Good then can you pour me a glass too?" Nyla glanced at Lovely with a hopeless face.

"Yeah," Lovely said walking over to the bar. I told you today was going to be hectic. I don't know why you wore those shoes, knowing they hurt your feet."

"Please, I can't be up in there looking like a hot mess at my own establishment. What kind of role model would I be?"

Lovely pulled out two glasses, poured them some white wine, and grabbed a bowl full of freshly washed grapes from the fridge walking back into the living room. "Thank God it's Friday." She placed the wine and bowl of grapes on the table and kicked off her shoes as well.

"How about a little relaxation music," Nyla turned on the music and played the Commodores, Three Times a Lady. "Oh yeah that is better. Now I can relax a little." Although she was not too far up in age, Nyla regularly enjoyed the sound of Motown music. Something her mother always played, as she was a little girl. "I remember when I was little my momma would play these records over and over, and sometimes I couldn't sleep unless I hear the sweet sound of Motown." She reminisced with her eyes closed and drifting into the sound of the music.

"Yeah I hear you girl. So what are we going to do tonight? Are we staying in or what?" Lovely asked Nyla curled up on the sofa barely awake.

"I don't know. I am tired, and my feet hurt. Why don't we just go out tomorrow?"

"Alright, well, I think I'm gonna go and take me a shower and relax then I guess we'll figure out what we're gonna be eating for dinner." Lovely walked back towards the bedroom with her glass of wine, and she went into the bathroom and turned the shower on as hot as she could stand it. As she began to get undressed, the steam from the shower filled the room. Lovely stepped into the shower letting the hot water trickle down her caramel skin, dripping from her erect nipples. *Ooh yeah,* she moaned as she thought of how good the water felt on her body, dazed in a relaxing mental state when the phone began to ring.

"Nyla, you got that?" She asked but heard no response. The phone continued to ring twice more and then stopped. Assuming that Nyla had answered the phone, she continued with her bath when the phone started to ring again. *Damn, who is on the phone?* She asked herself. "Nyla, you got the phone?" She asked again but still was no answer. Lovely turned off the water and stepped out of the shower wrapping herself in a towel rushing to answer the phone.

"Hello"

"Damn, you sure are hard to get a hold of. Don't you answer your phone?"

"Um, who is this?" Lovely did not recognize the sound of the man's voice.

"Oh, you forgot about me all ready huh. You must be really popular with the guys."

"Who is this?" She asked again losing her patients for whoever just interrupted her relaxation time.

"I'm sorry; it's Khalik; remember you met me about a week ago in the parking lot. I was driving the white BMW."

"Khalik, I didn't think you were going to call."

"Yeah, well I would have sooner but things have been a bit complicated lately but what do you say about having dinner with me tonight at Harry Caray's."

"Okay what time?" Lovely asked

"How about I pick you up at about 8:00"

"Alright, I'll see you at 8:00."

"Aiight, bye," Khalik said hanging up the phone.

Lovely hung up the phone and dived across the bed stretching out, exhaling. "Oh, what time is it?" She questioned aloud. *Its 6:45 so that means I only have an hour to get ready.* She thought. Lovely rose from the bed and went back into the bathroom to finish her shower. As she dried the water from her dripping naked body, she walked into the bedroom and pulled out a red-laced bra with the matching panties. She walked over to the mirror where she stood, admiring her own curves. *Damn I look good. Now what am I going to wear?*

Lovely looked into the closet and pulled out a black fitted Chanel dress with her favorite pair of black Chanel stilettos. As she finished dressing, she pulled her hair from the pinned bun, letting it fall, resting upon her shoulders. Lovely did not need much to be graceful. Her beauty was far beyond the makeup, which was why she wore none. *Now just a little Chanel No 5 and I am set to go.* Lovely looked up at the time once again. It was almost 8:00. She picked up her clutch and headed towards the front room. Nyla was stretched out upon the couch fast asleep. She headed towards the door easing it open to keep from waking Nyla and went down to wait for her date, but he was there waiting for her.

Standing next to the white BMW with an all-white Hugo Boss pinned stripped silk shirt and chino pants covering his ebony shaded skin smelling like a million bucks. Khalik was much of a street person but knew exactly how to turn on his suave and debonair when it came to a real woman. "Damn, you look just as good as I remember, only better."

Lovely smiled at the comment. "You don't look so bad yourself."

Khalik let out a light chuckle. "O.k. well let's go eat." He opened the door for Lovely before getting in the car his self.

The ride on the way to the restaurant was somewhat quiet but very flirtatious between the two of them. Lovely was quickly beginning to feel for Khalik and from then on she had a thing for him and was willing to spend all of her time with Khalik.

"So, you never did tell me what it was that you do." She asked him placing a piece of the grilled shrimp into her mouth.

"Well, you never said what it was that you do either. Now that we have finally gotten to sit, down and enjoy a nice dinner without our busy schedules conflicting. " He smiled, watching how sexy it was when she put the shrimp into her mouth, resting on her tongue.

"I asked you first."

"O.k. I do a little business for a lot of wealthy clients and a few lo-cal people as well."

"What kind of business?" She asked suspiciously as if she could smell the drugs in the air seeping from his pores.

"Let's just say that I give them what they need and leave them satis-fied," Going around answering the question directly.

"You not a gigolo are you?" She joked.

"Naw nothing like that, but that was a good one. So what is it that you do?" He quickly changed the subject and placed the attention back on her.

"Well, let's just say that I come from a very blessed family who takes care of a few wealthy people of their own."

"Alright fair enough, I guess we don't need to say no more. We both got dollars." He said smiling at her and eating his steak. As the night went on, they parted ways at nearly 9:30 in the evening. "Sorry we couldn't spend a little more time, but I got something important to handle right now; I just wanted to take a little break and have some dinner with you; get to know you a little."

"Yeah that's cool. I have to take care of some things myself, so I guess I'll talk to you…" Wondering when she would hear from him again.

"I'll call you tomorrow." He smiled at her again one last time before the night was over as he leaned into her and kissed her passion-ately. He sucked her lower lip ever so gently, right after his tongue left hers; leaving her breathless.

However, while he left her, breathless, Khalik was not the sweet and innocent one he seemed to be.

The time had passed, and Lovely and Khalik saw more and more of one another. Business was good, and her love life was only getting better. She picked up the phone and dialed Khalik's number but there was no answer, so she left a message. "Hi baby, it's me; I just wanted to call and talk to you before I lay down. You know I have my business trip tomorrow, and I will be gone for a couple of days. If I don't hear from you before I leave, then I guess I will talk to you, as soon as I get back." She hung up the phone. Lovely wanted to talk to him before leaving for her trip to Vegas but as usual at certain times of the night, she was unable to get a hold of him.

After months of dating, she still knew very little about whom he really was and what it was that he did for a living. Nevertheless, that did not bother her at all. She liked the suspense of the possibility of being with a made man or a millionaire. Lovely laid there in the bed continuing to wait for his call. Her eyes had become tight, and her vision blurred. She was tired. After lying there waiting on the call for thirty minutes, she finally fell asleep.

The morning crept in, and the alarm sounded with the creep of the sun through the blinds. Lovely wiped her eyes and awakened as she turned off the alarm clock. She picked up her phone from the nightstand to see if there were any missed calls but there was none. So lovely arose from the bed and began to get ready for her flight. In the midst of dressing, she wondered if she should call Khalik again. *I know he got the message. On the other hand, maybe he did not.* She thought as she contemplated whether she should call him so early or not. *If he wants to talk to me, then he will call me, I am sure he got my message.* She grabbed her bags and ticket for her flight and headed out of the front door.

12:00 midnight and the doorbell began to ring. Nyla awakened from a deep sleep and wondered if she was dreaming. She turned to look at the time and noticed it was late for someone to be ringing her doorbell this time of the night on a weekday. Everyone she knew had to get up for work in the morning, so she wondered who it could be. Nyla rose from the bed and reached the front door. She looked out of the peephole and could see that it was a man standing there but could not make out his face. "Who is it?" She yelled out to the man on the other side of the door.

"It's me, what's up?" Khalik answered.

Nyla opened the door slightly and saw Khalik standing there. "Hey what's up? What you doing here?" She asked with half her body hiding behind the door.

Where is your girl? Y'all sleeping? He asked.

"She left for that business trip already. You know; she had to go to Vegas to meet with some new clients we have been trying to go into opening up another spa. I thought she told you that." Nyla added.

"Oh yeah she did but I've been working so much the past few days that I haven't had the chance to talk to her. Why she didn't call me before she left any ways?"" He asked.

"She said she called you and left you a message, but you never called her back."

"Damn, I didn't get it. Well any ways when is she coming back?"

"She's going to be gone for a couple of days so if you want I'll tell her you came by."

"Yeah do that and tell her to hit me up?"

"Alright, good night." Nyla began closing the door when Khalik stopped her.

"Oh, I know it's late but do you mind if I use the bathroom real quick I have to pee bad as hell."

"Uh…." She hesitated a minute. "Yeah come on in." Nyla opened the door a little wider to let Khalik in then she flicked on the floor lamp next to the front entrance. "You already know where it is so you can go ahead and help yourself."

He walked into the apartment and headed towards the bathroom without even acknowledging her. Nyla walked into the kitchen and poured herself a glass of juice. As she stood there drinking she realized that she was only wearing a silk nighty with lace down the front to show off her breast. So she placed the cup down on the counter and headed towards the back room to grab her robe. As she walked through the hallway, Khalik was walking out of the bathroom, and they bumped into one another.

"Damn, my bad I didn't mean…. Sorry. You alright?" he asked.

"Yeah I'm ok. How about you?" She asked him.

"Yeah I'm good." They both stood there for a minute in the awkward moment. *Damn she smells good.* He thought as he looked into her eyes.

Um, he is so fine. Nyla thought. She looked back into his eyes and reached in to give him a kiss. Khalik moved his head away. "Oh my god I'm sorry. I don't know what I was thinking please…"

He grabbed the back of her head with both hands and kissed her lips. Khalik stuck his tongue deep into her mouth, and she started to let out a slight moan.

"Umm." She moaned. She stopped while he kissed her and pulled her lips from is.

He looked up at her, "What's up?"

Nyla pulled her nighty above her head and dropped it to the floor, revealing all of her nudeness. The light from the lamp in the front entrance captured the silhouette of her voluptuous body in the dark hallway. She walked past Khalik and stood in the front door of her room then she turned towards him, "Come, and get this pussy. I know you want it." She said as she walked into the dark room.

Hell yeah I want it. Khalik thought as he followed into the room behind her.

Nyla lay in the middle of the king-sized bed propped up against the oversized pillows with her leg's spread eagle and her knees slightly bent. She flicked on the bedside lamp so that they could get a better view of each other.

"Damn" Khalik said as he walked closer to the bed.

"Oh, you will be saying more than that once you get up in it. Not only is my pussy pretty, but it tastes just as good as it looks and it feels like you have walked out of heaven. When I get through you won't even have an appetite for nothing but this pussy."

Khalik pulled his white t-shirt above his head and began to take off the rest of his clothes. He was hard as a rock and enticed just by looking at the curvaceous figure and the pussy staring him dead in the face. As much as he started to like Lovely, she had not put out but a couple of times, and he was beginning to wonder why even bother. He was a young man, and he needed it on the regular.

Khalik climbed upon the bed and kissed Nyla on her belly button. He figured if he smelled anything that smelled like fish than he would be able to tell from there. However, he did not. Nyla smelled just as good as she looked from head to toe. He lied down on his stomach in between her legs and pulled them further apart. Khalik had no problem pleasing any woman because he knew that if you pleased the woman first, then she would be yours all night long. You could have your way with her repeatedly. Besides, he liked the way pussy smelled and loved the way it felt along his tongue.

Nyla looked down at Khalik. He stared up at her the placed three fingers inside of her moving in and out of her vagina. Nyla began to moan while still keeping her eyes on him. His eyes were locked with hers, and he stuck out his tongue and began stroking her clit. Her pussy became wetter as he stroked her. She could tell by the look in his eyes that he had wanted to taste her all night long. After getting the pussy, good and wet, Khalik could tell as he lifted up that she was ready to be fucked.

He turned her over on her stomach and leaned in behind her ear and whispered, "Stick that ass up in the air and let me in." Nyla arched her back, stuck out her ass, and spread her legs apart. "Yeah, just like that." Khalik rubbed his fingers along the inside of her pussy to make sure it was still wet. It was like a faucet. He spat his hands a little and rubbed all eight inches of his dick then he placed it inside of her. Nyla screamed and moaned to the strokes of his hips.

Khalik thrust inside and out until finally he was ready to explode. Just before, he pulled out and turned her back over on her back. "Let me see you swallow." He grabbed his dick and stroked it to Nyla playing with her pussy and rubbing her breast. "I'm 'bout to cum." She pushed his hands off and grabbed his dick and stroked it until he exploded in her mouth, letting the cum slide down to the back of her throat. He had released his self and they both were satisfied. Khalik then rose from the bed. "I got to go." He said to Nyla.

"Yeah and I have to get up for work in the morning, so I guess this is it." She responded.

"Yeah, I got you. Don't worry were good. I won't tell if you won't." She confirmed.

"Yeah, aiight. Let me get the number to your cell, so I can hit you up." He said.

Nyla wrote down her cell phone number and gave it to Khalik. He placed it in his pocket and headed towards the front door. Nyla followed behind him. "See you."

He turned towards her and gripped her ass once more. "Aiight, I can let myself out. "I'll holler at you." He opened the door and walked out. Nyla had just betrayed her best friend in the whole world, and she did not feel any remorse.

Lovely stepped off the plane and headed home from her business trip. She picked up her cell phone and called Nyla but there was no answer, so she left a message. "Hey I guess you're working hard so I will see you at home in a little while. I wanted to let you know that I just got in, and I am going to ride down to see my uncle before I come home. Talk to you soon."

She pulled up to her Uncle Jimmy's house and noticed a few extra cars than usual in the driveway. However, it was no surprise because her uncle knew everyone around. She walked up towards the door and noticed the white BMW parked in front. She thought nothing of it. Lovely rang the doorbell then walked into the house.

The guard stood there and spoke. "How's it going Lovely?"

"Alright, just came to see my uncle is he here?" she asked but already knew that he was.

"Yeah he's in the conference room." The guard replied.

Lovely walked down to the conference room and knocked on the door. She opened it up before waiting to hear him answer. "Hey!"

"Oh baby girl come on in." Jimmy said. Lovely walked in, went over to her uncle, and gave him a hug.

Just then, Hassan noticed who she was, but she had not noticed him. *Damn, this is his daughter.* He thought. He was surprised because neither him, nor Khalik knew of any family that Jimmy had.

"This is my niece lovely for those who don't know who she is so that means to keep your hands to yourself." Jimmy said to all his runners in the room as he could see them trying not to look at her beauty.

Just then, Khalik walked into the room and instantly made eye contact with her. He was surprised to see lovely standing there. *What in the hell is she doing here?* He thought to his self.

"Khalik this is my niece Lovely. Baby girl this is one of my best men right here, him and Hassan over there," Pointing to him at the other end of the table.

"What's up?" Hassan said as he nodded his head and looked away as if he had never seen her before.

Khalik walked over to the table and sat down. "Nice to meet you lovely." He said.

"Yeah you too." She replied. Lovely was just as shocked to see the two of them as they were to see her. "You know I just stopped by, but I am tired, so I'm gonna wait for you in the upstairs room until you get through with your meeting." She reached down and kissed him on the cheek then walked out, staring at Khalik as she exited the room with her back to her uncle.

"Alright baby girl. I'll be finished shortly." Jimmy said to her.

Lovely awakened from the daydream. She was still taken away just from the thought of the first-time Khalik had kissed her. She had to figure out what was going on and why her uncle had been killed and as much as she did not want to believe it, she knew that they were the ones that committed such a crime against him. Khalik was the man whom she once fell in love with and in some ways still cared for but could no longer be with. Now she had to focus on revenge for her uncle's death. The outcome of her vengeance was not going to be so lovely.

Chapter Six
The Key

Back at the precinct later that day, Detective Smith searched the database for anything he could find on Jimmy that could possibly lead him to the key that was hidden in the safe. Then he remembered that some of the officers had gathered a bunch of Jimmy's mail for evidence. The mail was lying on top of the cabinet by the picture were the safe was. As he searched through, he found a letter from the Chicago National Bank, one of the most popular high-end banks in Chicago where only the rich and well off keeps their big money.

Whitman walked over, handing Smith a cup of coffee. "So did you find anything?"

"Yeah, as a matter of fact, I went through some of the mail we had for evidence and found out that he banked at the Chicago National." Smith confirmed.

"So that means that we can find that safety deposit box to match the key we found." Whitman said putting two and two together.

"Exactly, let's go."

Detectives Whitman and Smith got into the cop car and hurried to Chicago National Bank. As they pulled up Smith turned off the car and turned to look at Whitman.

"Now, what we do is go in here and act as if we have this case under investigation, as we do, and we need to confiscate all assets of the victim."

"Yeah, alright let's just hope, they don't need a search warrant. You know how these uppity ass big shots are." Whitman reminded Smith about how things such as this can be blown out of proportion when it comes to the high end parts of town; people believing their better than the rest of the world.

"Our search warrant is right here, these badges. Now let's go." Smith said as they both got out of the car and headed towards the door of the bank.

As they walked into the front door, a man walking by wearing an expensive suit with a clean-cut and nicely trimmed but long beard walked by slightly bumping into Smith.

"Oh excuse me sir." The man said tapping Smith on the shoulder without even looking up and acknowledging him at all. As he walked off, he realized whom he had just bumped into, but continued to walk on without acknowledging Smith and quickly got into his car. *Hey, it's me, look; there are two cops coming in. I want you to do me a favor and let me know what they wanted.*

Smith stopped. *Ass* hole. He turned around and looked as the man walked away with his head down. *He looks very familiar to me, where could I have seen him?* Smith thought to himself but then quickly remembered why he was there.

They walked over to the counter.

"Hi officer my name is Tom is there something I can help you with?" The clerk at the front counter asked.

"Yes, we need to know if you have a man by the name of Jimmy Johnson that bank here?" Whitman asked the clerk.

As Smith and Whitman asked the clerk for information on Jimmy, the manager could overhear the officers as he hung up the phone with Jose and decided to walk over.

"I'll take it from here Tom."

"Hello, I'm Billy, the manager over here at Chicago National. How can I be of assistance to you officer's today?"

"Well Billy, we are conducting a murder investigation, and we need to know if you have a fellow by the name of Jimmy Johnson that bank here?"

"Well, yes, Mr. Johnson is one of our most valued customers.

Is there a problem?" Billy asked with a look of concern on his face. Nervous from the two officers asking questions.

"Like we said we are investigating a murder. I don't know if you watch the local news here Mr. Billy but Mr. Johnson was killed in his home just recently, and we need to confiscate all of his assets to be sure that there isn't anything that may help us to find out who may have killed him." Smith told him, changing his voice to sound as if he was there to investigate.

"Oh my God, I had no idea. I will be more than happy to help you, uh, would you happen to have a warrant?" Billy said looking as if there was something to hide.

"Warrant." Whitman looked at Smith with a smile as Smith let out a light chuckle. They both turned and looked at Billy.

Smith leaned over towards Billy whispering to him. "Tell me something Billy, what kind of business did Mr. Jonson say he was in?"

"Business." Billy began to sweat from the nervousness. He did not need any cops searching around the bank costing him his job from allowing a drug dealer to have illegal accounts held there.

"Yes business. You see, the way I look at it is you either give us what we need, or we get a warrant and shut down the entire bank for investigation for holding money from illegal drug purchases. Now you don't want that do you Billy?"

"No, no sir right this way. Follow me."

Smith and Whitman followed Billy into the back where the safety deposit boxes were.

"Mr. Johnson closed out his account with us weeks ago, but he did still keep a deposit box that he had for his niece, Janae Luvell as another authorized person to have access to the deposit box."

Billy pulled out the box and placed it on the table where both detectives Smith and Whitman were standing by.

"By any chance would this be the key that goes to this box?" Smith pulled the key out of his pocket and showed it to Billy.

"Uh, yes sir this is one of our keys. Let me see if the numbers match." Billy read the numbers on the deposit box and looked at the numbers on the key. "Yep this is the key. Mr. Johnson had only one key issued to him, and it appears that this is it."

"Leave us alone for a minute." Whitman told Billy showing him out of the room as if he was running the place.

They both sat there looking at the box. Staring at it as if they had no idea. What would be next? Smith took the key and unlocked the box, lifting it up to discover that there was nothing but money, all in 100-dollar bills.

"How much you think it is?" Whitman asked.

"Well there's only one way to find out." Smith opened the door and saw Billy standing not too far from it. He gave him a look that Billy immediately understood it was for him to come and see what the cops had wanted.

"Yes sir."

Smith closed the door behind Billy as he walked into the room. "About how much would you say is in this safety deposit box?"

"There are 10,000,000 in there, I know because Mr. Johnson came to me personally to set this up for him."

"Well Billy we are gonna need to confiscate every penny so if you would be a good sport and bag this up for us, we'll appreciate it." Whitman looked him in his eyes with the most serious face. "Maybe we'll throw you a little something for being such a big help and uh; we will keep this between us."

"Yeah since you helped us out so much then we will be sure not to get the bank involved." Smith confirmed to him sending a relief his way as he sighed from fearing the thought of the officers investigating the bank.

"Yes, sir, and thank you officer's, I will get this together for you as quickly as possible."

As Billy placed the money into a bag for them, Smith grabbed the key and placed it back into his pocket. *I don't think they will be missing this.*

Billy finished placing all the money from the safety deposit box in the bag and handed it to Smith. He reached in and pulled out a stack of money giving him a portion of it to keep him quiet.

"Thank you so much." Billy looked at Smith and reached out his hand to grab the money.

"You just remember what we said and everything will be fine." Smith gave him the money, and they headed out of the bank. Never again did it hit Smith about the man who he had been bumped by when entering the bank.

Billy picked up the phone, as soon as he was sure that Detectives Smith and Whitman had gone. "Yeah, they were asking questions about Jimmy Johnson, and they had a key to his safety deposit box. They confiscated it all, but get this; it was 10,000,000 in the box, and they said they needed everything for evidence. I had no choice but to give it to them."

"Alright, thanks man." Jose said to Billy as he hung up the phone.

As Whitman and Smith walked out of the bank the black Lexus pulled up and watched them as they got into their car; closely watching and following them from far behind.

Smith and Whitman drove down to the same field where they had taken Hassan to convince him to get rid of Jimmy. "Now all we have to do is hide the money somewhere out here where only the two of us would know where it is and when everything is all taken care of with those fucking greedy niggers, then we get the money and split it straight down the middle."

"Alright, sounds fair." They got out of the car, "Now, where should we bury the money?" Whitman asked Smith.

"Wait, it looks like a car is coming." As the Lexus got a little closer, they began to notice, when they both got back into the car.

Realizing that they had noticed the car sitting there, the Lexus drove off.

"Do you think that someone was following us?" Whitman asked.

"Look at you, you're paranoid. Nobody knows about this money except for Jimmy, and he is dead, so now it is all ours. All we have to do is keep a low profile for a little while and wait until everything's blows over."

"Alright, well I think it may be clear so let's hurry up and find a spot before someone else comes by."

As they got back out of the car, they began to look around quickly for a spot where they can remember exactly where they left it when they return for it later.

Smith noticed a big rock sitting over by a bunch of grass and a few bushes. "This will work perfectly. We just dig the hole under the rock and bury the money there."

Whitman and Smith quickly dug up the hole and buried the money in the same bag that they had gotten from the bank. "Well, now all we have to do is wait, and we are home free." Whitman looked over at Smith. Both gave a smile and shook hands as they had conjured up a perfect plan and gotten away with it. However, neither of them could help but to think if the other would be true to his word, or would things get a little more complicated. Could either of them trust one another was the question.

Detective Smith pulled up to his house where he walked in from the precinct noticing his wife, Shanell, sitting on the chase drinking a glass of wine and reading a magazine. He looked around the room and walked into towards the bar pouring himself a drink.

"Long day at work," Shanell asked, not getting a response back "Can I get you something?"

He sipped a bit of the Hennessy and walked over to her where she sat looking up at him. "Why haven't you made dinner?"

"Well I thought you weren't coming home until later so I thought I would just relax a bit before I started dinner."

"Relax a little," He repeated looking at Shanell with a vengeful face. He reached his hand back and slapped her across the face shedding blood from her nose and quickly bruising her cheek. Shanell let out a whimper, grabbing the side of her face. No sooner than the force came a great deal of anger as Smith grabbed Shanell by the hair and pulled her off the chaise, kicking her repeatedly in the stomach. "Now, get your useless ass in that kitchen and make me some dinner." He said as he walked off.

"You bastard you're going to pay for what you have done, all these years and not once have you felt any remorse for your actions."

"Remorse, you wanna talk about remorse, if it weren't for me, you would still be slumming with those lowlife drug dealing niggers. Let's face it; you would probably be dead or on drugs, maybe even selling your body if I hadn't felt sorry for you." He walked up to her and looked her in the eyes. "You owe me your life."

Shanell spit in his face, "Fuck you, I don't need you and when he gets out he's gonna kill you."

"Kill me, kill me, you nigger loving bitch" He grabbed her by her hair again pulling her up from the ground and punched her in the stomach. Shanell screamed as he lifted her face, "Get out, oh baby he's never getting out and as for Jimmy, I made sure that he never sets foot anywhere else; he lays deep in a casket. Not to mention the wad of money I got in the process."

"Jimmy" Shanell looked as if she was in disbelief, "Jimmy's dead?" Smith looked at her and took another sip of his Hennessy. "You killed him, you sick fuck you killed him didn't you? Why did you do it, huh? It wasn't bad enough that you already screwed-up everything else, why did you do it?" Shanell yelled.

Shanell was the only white woman whom Jimmy had trusted with anything. She had been working with him for years and was pretty much his top bitch with a good strong hustle and was willing to help get rid of anybody that got in their way if he needed her to. Shanell and Jimmy kept their relationship strictly business. The fact that she could easily blend in with the rest of the corporate world without being suspicious was exactly what he needed to get his hustle through to the right people.

Shanell had fallen for someone else, who she loved, someone very dear and near to Jimmy. She was always loyal and for that, he kept her around. It was all good until Smith stepped in and decided he had seen something he wanted. He made sure if Jimmy hadn't cooperated and gave him some of the profits that he made on the streets from selling drugs to some of the most prominent people in Chicago, then he would make everyone around him pay, and he meant it. Smith proved this to him once and would soon do it again before plotting to take his life.

Smith pulled into the parking lot next to Jimmy. "Jimmy, Jimmy, how's it hanging?" He said as they both stood outside their cars for their monthly exchange of money. Jimmy paid Smith 5,000 a month just to keep from going to jail and losing everything that he has built.

Jimmy gave him a deep look and handed him the money.

"What, no greeting for someone who's keeping your black ass out of prison. You see that's what's wrong with your kind you don't know when to expect someone who's trying to help you."

Just as Smith finished his sentence, the door to Jimmy's car opened and a woman climbed out. "Jimmy baby we have to go there is an important matter that needs your attention."

"Whoa, what do we have here? Is this you Jimmy? Man where have you been hiding her? Smith looked at the woman with a lust in his eyes. "What do you say you come and take a ride with me, huh sugar?"

She looked at him with a disgusted look upon her face. "No thanks, you're not my type."

"Oh, o.k. Miss…"

"Shanell"

"Shanell, well Jimmy I guess I will be seeing you later, there are definitely some things we need to reconsider. Miss Shanell." Smith said walking closely up to Shanell to shake her hand, but she quickly got back into the car.

Smith walked away and got into his car slowly driving off, giving Jimmy a long stare.

"Sorry motherfucker can't make enough money on your own so you want to take my shit, Bastard." Jimmy spoke his thoughts aloud as he proceeded to get into the car and drive off. He knew that what they had to reconsider had everything to do with Shanell. It was only a matter of time before he had to let her go and as much as he hated to, let alone paying Smith every month, he had to do what he had to do.

Jimmy sat at the head of the table surrounded by everyone who worked for him. They sat and ate dinner as Jimmy talked about their next moves to expand further and how he needed some of his guys to take over and get things started out in Cali.

"Jamel I'm gonna need you and Shanell to get out there in Cali and do your thing. I got a few boys out there who waiting to show you how shit goes down there, and then we should be set. It's supposed to be some paper out there." Jimmy expressed

"Shit, you know me I'm going to put it down, straight up." Jamel said shoving food into his mouth.

"Now……" The doorbell followed by pounding on the door interrupted Jimmy. "Who the fuck is it?" He yelled out to one of the guards as he walked towards the foyer to get the door.

"Well, well, well, what do we have here? It looks like a little meeting. Did we interrupt something?" Smith said sarcastically as he bursts through the door past the guard.

"What the fuck you want motherfucker?" Jamel stood up with an

AK47 next to him.

"Jimmy, Jimmy, my boy, you better put your hounds on a leash. I would hate to have to take them down to the precinct and let some of my guys get more acquainted. They like fresh meat." Smith replied

"Alright man, look. What are you doing here I'm trying to eat with my family?" Jimmy asked

"Well I wouldn't exactly call this family time, but hey, whatever. You remember I told you we needed to have a little talk to reconsider some things. Well now is that time." Smith began to circle around the long dining table then stopped right behind Shanell. As he circled, Jimmy's army of men stood up ready for Jimmy to say when. Smith placed his hands upon Shanell's shoulders, rubbing them.

"Muthafucka" Jamel rushed towards Smith and before Jimmy could stop him. He punched Smith in the face, shedding blood from his nose and mouth, knocking him to the ground.

"Jamel, what the hell, back up. What you trying to do man do you know who the fuck this is?"

Smith wiped his hand across his face and seen the blood. He picked his self up from the ground and looked at Jamel. "You done made a big mistake boy. You gone have to get down on your knees and apologize right now, or we're gonna have an even bigger problem."

"What nigga you think I give a fuck 'bout your threat's motherfucker. You're not anything but a crooked ass law," Jamel yelled out in a rage.

"Jimmy I think you need to remind this nigga that I am not to be fucked with." Smith said looking jimmy deep into his eyes.

"What!" Jamel was stunned. This law had a lot of nerves to come up in a house full of black men and call out the word nigga. The rest of the room was silent, but you could see the anger in the expressions upon their faces.

"Look Smith, your way out of line now. Shit this is my house. You got what you wanted now I am asking you to leave. We can talk about whatever it is some other time." Jimmy said

"Oh but you see I haven't gotten everything that I wanted, there's still one more thing left, and I intend to collect before I go." He looked over at Shanell. Shanell looked up at Jamel. Jamel charged back at Smith, but before he could reach him, Smith pulled out his gun and shot him in the leg.

"Oh shit!" Jamel screamed out.

"Now maybe you'll sit there and listen." He continued to point the gun at Jamel.

"What the fuck are you doing?" Jimmy yelled to Smith.

"Enough with the small talk. You know what I want, and I want it now." Smith pointed the gun at Shanell "Now get up sweet cakes. You're coming with me."

Shanell had a surprised look upon her face. "Get the hell off me."

"Jimmy what the hell man are you just going to let this crooked ass law come up in here and shoot me then take Shanell?" Jamel said lying on the floor bleeding from the bullet that went straight through his leg.

Smith grabbed Shanell by her arm and pulled her up from the chair. "Now, what I want you to do is tell your hounds they had better sit." Talking to Jimmy "If anybody tries anything when I leave here, this whole operation is going to be shut down and this pretty piece of pussy, well, I don't know what might happen to her. I would hate to come and have to recover all of your bodies from this nice house, lying cold and dead in the morgue where your mama's and wives can't identify you." Smith turned around facing Jamel "As for you; I think you might want to stay the fuck out of my way before I have your ass rot in jail."

Jamel stared him deep in the eyes as Smith grabbed Shanell and walked towards the door. The guys stood there looking, not believing that Jimmy just let this white law come and regulate in his house, disrespecting everything that he stood for.

"Oh yeah, we'll meet at the usual spot and don't be late." Smith told Jimmy. They walked out of the house, and Smith put Shanell in the back seat of the police car where she could not get out. He got into the car and drove off making a phone call. "Yeah were all set so just keep your eye out." Smith had been watching jimmy and knew exactly who everyone in his crew was, especially Jamel. His plan was to keep jimmy around to continue his monthly payments but Smith had decided that Jamel would be a problem, and he was going to take care of it before it began.

"Look we have got to get you to a hospital," Jimmy said to Jamel

"Man get the fuck off me Jimmy. I can take myself to the hospital, besides you just sold out. I don't need you for shit. Come on Mike, let's roll." Jamel and his closest runner walked out towards the door. As they headed to the car, two police cars pulled up behind his car blocking his way. "What the hell is going on?" Jamel stood there bleeding wondering what was about to happen.

"Jamel nice to see you again" The officer said. It was a face Jamel had not seen in years. An officer who booked him up on weed charges when he was younger. "I see you took a step up from selling weed. Now you're in the big time."

"Look man I don't know what you're talking 'bout. Any ways, what are you doing here?"

"You know exactly what I'm doing here." The officer opened up his car and pulled out bags of cocaine.

"Yo that shit is not mine. What the fuck you trying to do. You motherfuckers trying to set me up" Jamel said angrily.

The officer and his partner grabbed Jamel and cuffed him, throwing him in the back of the police car. They left Mike standing there scared, not knowing what to do. Jamel was taken to a nearby field and beating half the death then the officers took him down to the precinct and booked him in. Saying they found him lying on the side of the road beaten, and he had drugs all in the car. Jamel would spend years in jail before he would ever see the outside of prison again, Shanell, or the unborn baby that she carried.

"Look, I don't answer to you bitch, besides it's none of your business what I do and the next time you raise your voice in my house, I'm gonna kill you myself."

"Oh, so that's how you did it; you paid someone to do your dirty work for you so there is no way that it traces back to you. Well, the blood is all over you, no matter who did it; you are going to pay for what you have done, for everything, you hear me? You sick bastard." As Shanell kept yelling, Smith pulled out his gun and shoved it in her mouth as he grabbed her by her hair.

"You bitch, say one more word, and I'm gonna splatter your fucking brains all over these walls." Shanell starts to cry, begging him to stop. "Oh, what's wrong is it too much of a mouthful? What, you don't have anything else you want to say, huh." Smith kept the metal piece in her mouth moving it around. "What's the matter? I thought you liked having things in your mouth."

She closed her eyes as tears ran down her face. Smith looked her in the eyes, "If I find out that you've been saying things around here to people and putting your nose where it doesn't belong I will kill you. You understand me?" Shanell shook her head, "Good" Smith said as he pistol-whipped her across the face letting her body drop to the floor unconscious, he walked out.

As the hours passed, Shanell finally came to and immediately headed towards the bedroom searching through Smith's things in the boxes on top of the closet. She found what she was looking for, his backup gun, and lying in the box next to it were the bullets. Shanell ran towards the front door in a frantic, angry, and confused all at the same time as she hopped into her car and sped off down the street.

Whitman awoke to the sound of pounding on his door. He got up from his couch that he had fallen asleep on and answered it.

"Who is it?" He yelled out.

"It's me Shanell; I need your help. Please open the door."

"Look. What are you doing here? Where is Smith? If he finds you here he's gonna fucking kill you."

"He beat me up pretty bad this time, and he was so drunk. I guess he left because by the time I woke up he was gone so I ran out of the house as quick as I could, but I have nowhere to go." Shanell was quivering as tears rolled down her bruised face. She still had bruises on her from the last time he beat on her, which was only a few days before.

"So you come here? I cannot help you. You need to go home before he finds you."

"I can't. Look, I just need some money, so I can get a ticket out of here and maybe a descent change of clothes and some food. Something to get me by for a little while, please," Shanell barged her way into the door. Will you help me?"

"Yeah, just wait here and I'll see what I have." Whitman walked over to the bedroom where he picked up the phone and dialed Smith's number, but there was no answer."

"Not so fast Asshole." Shanell said. Whitman turned around and looked Shanell deep into her eyes. She could see the fear, as if she had set him up, and she could tell that he was not expecting it. He gazed back at her with a wicked smirk on his face. "What the hell are you doing?"

"Well you see when Smith told me about Jimmy, I knew that you had something to do with it too. Apparently, Smith thought he could get away with it and so did you."

"Whatever the fuck you're doing, you are gonna get yourself into some serious shit. Do you know who I am? Huh, I'm the law and I'll put your ass in jail for the rest of your life bitch. But then again, I won't have to cause when Smith hears about this, he's going to kill you his self."Whitman said not even caring at all that she had a gun to his head.

"Like you did Jimmy Johnson?"

"What, who the fuck...." Whitman was startled by the words he had heard. *How could this be?* His partner betrayed him, set him up. "How the fuck did you know about that?"

"Fucking ass hole, how do you think; your partner sold your ass out." Shanell told him with aggression deep in her voice making Whitman question his partners' sincerity. "Yeah, that's right, he told me everything, and your ass is going down. It only takes one trip to the precinct; believe me, he would never rat on his self; you're as good as busted."

"Look I'll give you the money just put the gun down." Whitman tried reasoning with her, barely looking at her. He focused his attention on the gun trying to make sure she did not use it.

"Take a closer look into my eyes. My life has been hell, and as long as you have helped him, you are a part of that as well, so now I am gonna kill you."

Whitman's eyes got wider. He became vulnerable to the situation. The thought of Smith betraying him sickened his stomach; so sick that he began to throw up right there in front of her, landing on her feet.

"You are a sick bastard, where's the fucking money?" She began waving the gun and finally started to pistol whip him with it.

"What money? I don't know what you're talking about." Still leaning over with throw up dripping from his lips and smeared across his cheek as he wiped his mouth with the sleeve of his shirt. "Look, I'll give some money if that is all you need, just get the gun out of my fucking face."

"Well, you must have forgotten that I am the one with the gun which means I am the one who calls all the shots, and if you don't give me some money then I am gonna shoot you." Shanell began to point the gun directly at his head grabbing him by the hair. "I am gonna ask you one more time, and if you don't tell me where it is or where I can get it, I will kill you right now." She was desperate and ready to make that escape from him, all she needed was some money to get there and the only person she could go to was him.

"O.k. just let me get cleaned up, and I'll take you to get some money. I have some stashed, me and Smith, but this has got to be between me and you."

Shanell walked him into the other room where the bathroom was and let Whitman clean the barf off his face. While holding him at gunpoint she walked him outside and forced him into the police car, driving off with the gun still pointing at his head. Whitman drove her to the field where he and Smith had buried the money. They parked and then got out of the car.

"Where is it? Take me to it now." Shanell said with the gun still pointed at Whitman.

"Alright, it's over here buried under this rock." He walked over towards the rock and picked it up placing it to the side. "I'm going to need something to dig it up with."

"Use your hands."

"What?" Whitman looked back at her; Shanell was serious, and she was not going to budge. He had to figure out something before she tried to kill him and take the money. "Look, could you at least see if there is a big stick or something so that I can get the dirt out?"

Shanell turned her back to see if there was a large stick ling around when before she knew it Whitman grabbed her from behind, placing her in a headlock, choking her. The gun fell from her hands as she struggled to get him off her. She kicked back her leg and hit him in the groin. Whitman folded, releasing her from the headlock he had her in. Shanell dived to the ground and grabbed the gun, but Whitman had gotten on top of her. They struggled and wrestled with the gun. Finally, as Whitman lay on top of her Shanell could grasp the gun harder, placed her fingers inside the trigger, and pulled. She shot Whitman in the chest.

Whitman paused, shocked and in pain from the bullet hitting him. He took a last look into her eyes and fell on top of her. Shanell pushed him off. His blood covered her hands and the front of her shirt. She picked herself up from the ground and looked at Whitman again, firing once more into his chest. Making sure, he was dead. She turned ad began to dig up the dirt.

Finally, Shanell saw the bag that the money lay in buried beneath the dirt. She continued to dig up the rest and pulled the bag from the ground. As she opened it, she began to see large amounts of money in stacks, pulling it out. *Oh, my God it has to be at least a few thousand in here, maybe even a million.* She thought. Shanell placed the money back into the bag and got into the car, driving off.

Chapter Seven

The Connect

Khalik thought about Hassan and how easy it was for him to be attached to that life. He wondered if they had not committed that first crime against his dad. Where would their lives be, what would have become of them? They were young, and they would have done anything to get out of that situation.

Interrupted from his thoughts and memory of the past, "Khalik Johnson, bunk your junk boy, your time is almost here." It was his cellmate keeper.

Khalik looked up from the daze that he was in while laying on his bunk thinking about old times and the years he had spent in prison. Keeper was an older gangster who had gotten his name because he had been in prison twice as long as Khalik and a lot of others for murdering a state judge, his lawyer, and their families. He said he killed the judge for sentencing him to jail for two years for robbing a convenience store; keeper claimed that his sentence was unfair and the lawyer was not even on his side, so he killed him too. He figured if he had to be taken away from his family, and then he wanted the same for the people who took him, so he killed their families as well. Keeper was supposed to be on death row, but they could not prove that he actually committed the crime himself, so the state sentenced him to life in prison without the possibility of parole.

"Hey Keeper, what's up man? Where have you been?" Khalik asked as if there were so many places they could go.

"Oh youngster you know me I was just sitting down trying to watch a little news, keeping up with what's going on in the world since I'm not gonna ever see the outside again," Looking at Khalik with a desperate stare.

"Shit, man, you know the fucked up thing is that after only three years It seems like I'm not gonna ever get out, shit, I still can't believe it. The way those motherfuckers set me up, I feel like I'm going to die in here with you niggas, no offense."

Keeper raised his brow and looked at Khalik as if he did catch offense, but did not say anything. "None taken, if I had to do this all over again I'm not so sure that I would've done nothing different; that's probably why they need to keep my black ass locked up. The world isn't ready for an old school nigga like me man, I'm prepared to destroy some shit at all cost, and I don't give a fuck about anything or nobody but my family. Speaking of family, are you going to try to find out what happened to yours?"

"Man Keep, honestly I don't have any family and I'm not so sure I won't run into somebody that put me here. I'm not trying to come back to this motherfucker man." Khalik did not speak on his family to anyone in prison. He felt as if there was no trust between him and those in his position. These were murderers and sex offenders. He did not care about none of them so why would he tell them anything.

"Yeah, I feel that. You'll figure out what to do youngster, just keep your head up, Shit you know what I say, go back and claim what's yours. I'm gonna go to the yard and shoot some ball, show these young niggas how to do it. Later," Keeper walked out of the cell.

Khalik continued to think about how he had been set up. These were some of the hardest nights within these prison walls. There were so many people that he had unfinished business with, and he could not just let things go. He had to get his revenge; most importantly the one person who he trusted with his life had promised he would always be there was gone. The other person who he trusted and thought was down, but even he had become unknown to him. Khalik had made a mental list of all who had placed death upon him, who had deceived him, who had forgotten him, and ultimately who had been untrue to their words and undying love for him. Everyone was gone and there was nothing he could do to bring him or her back but the two who did remain had to pay, and he would make sure of it.

"Johnson," mail up. The guard placed the mail into the slot of the cell door as it fell to the floor. Khalik picked the letter up, standing and staring at it, not knowing what it was or whom it was from. This was probably the only letter that he would receive in the mail like this since he had not gotten anything the whole time he was there. He was almost scared of what he had missed and knew nothing about all these years. The fear in his heart came from not knowing what he would feel once he was released, the revenge and pain that had been building up inside of him for three years.

He looked to read the name on the envelope. It was addressed *John Doe*. Khalik opened the envelope and begin to read. *"For three years you've waited and for three years I've plotted, but soon it will be time."*

The letter was quick and to the point. There was no need for Khalik to question or even wonder what it meant without knowing where it came from. His heart was full of revenge and no matter what or who stood in the way they would become a part of that revenge. Khalik could remember the importance of wanting to be the big man in Chicago as a youngster out there on the streets.

Even though Hassan was always the initiator in most all the situations they got into, without Jose they would not have been able to get passed that street robbing and stealing. But instead they were moving weight and became who they were, two of the most feared, respected, and known dealers in Chicago.

Thinking back to that day, that very conversation between him and Jose, he started to remember how good it felt Jose to say those words. To tell him that they would be moving up to the real stuff, no more penny pinch in' and petty hustling.

Khalik pulled up at the stop light with the music turned up, rattling the trunk of the car when the phone rang. "Hello," He answered, "What's up Jose?"

"Meet me on the corner of 67ᵗʰ and Wolcott." Jose told Khalik.

"Aiight, I'll be there in a minute." Khalik pulled up on the corner of 67ᵗʰ and Wolcott. Jose was already there waiting in his Chevy, as Khalik pulled up and parked, Jose got out his car and walked towards him.

"What's up man? Where are you coming from?" He asked as they gave each other daps

"Shit, you know, just riding 'round trying to get into something. What's up with you?" Khalik asked leaning against his cherry red Cadillac.

"I wanted to holler at you 'bout something."

"Oh yeah, what?"

"I know we have been doing our thing out here on the streets here and there, but remember I was telling you that I got an uncle in Mexico, who works for this Mexican Mob boss named Chavez, who runs this drug cartel, right."

"Yeah, what up?" Khalik continuously asked again leaning with his arms crossed and interested in what Jose had to tell him.

"Check this out, I talked to my uncle, and he says he talked to Chavez 'bout doing some work with him, moving a little weight down here. I mean, Shit, Hassan's right; we won't be able to be robbing motherfuckers forever." Jose expressed, knowing that it all started as a part-time hustle for them; full-time for Hassan despite his constant talk about him being too good.

"Hell yeah man, I'm with it. That's what we need right there any ways." Khalik said getting excited without even hearing all that Jose had to say.

"Well, you see; the only catch is that he might not want to deal with both of us, so since my uncle is hooking me up, and then I'm gonna go and talk to him first and see if everything is cool. If everything is all-good, we'll go down there and meet him. I hope that we in there and we can get started on this shit. You feel me?"

"Hell yeah, I'm feeling that. Your boy is definitely feeling that." Khalik expressed as him and Jose clasped and shook hands.

"Well, look, I'm going to keep you posted I just wanted to catch up with you and let you know what was going down. I got some stuff to do, so I'll get up with you later."

"Aiight then, bet that up. Good looking out." Khalik said to Jose as they clasped hands once again and both got into their cars; driving off.

Hassan and Khalik sat back lying on the white sandy beaches of Cancun Mexico sipping some Hennessy while listening to the sounds of the crystal blue Caribbean waters. "Damn Khalik this shit right here is what a nigga needed man."

"Yeah, now that we got a little money to hold us down is cool Jose got that connect. This shit we got from Jimmy is going to run out eventually man and in order to live like this, we have to keep it going. And I know these fucking Mexicans 'bout they paper."

"Yeah man I feel you, but the only problem is that if these motherfuckers don't trust us. They are not going to be so quick to make a deal with a nigga. We'll be mess with the big timers out here, and they'll try to string our black asses up before they just do business with us." Hassan said.

"What about the connect that Jimmy had, did you find out which one of those Mexican Mafia's he got that his dope from? Jimmy always had his stuff legit with the dope, that's why he made so much money because that shit was the truth." Khalik continued

"Naw, I overheard him talking one day and the man's name is

Chave. But I'm not really sure."

"Any ways, when is Jose supposed to meet up with us? I thought he said he was taking the next flight out. What's up?" Hassan asked.

"You know his grandmother is in the hospital, and the doctors say she might be getting worse, so that's why he said to go ahead and come down here. He told me that if he couldn't make it for the reason she got any worse, then we should just handle it without him and keep him posted until we get back."

As Khalik and Hassan continued to talk, there was a man who walked over and approached them.

"Excuse me I couldn't help but to overhear you talking, and I think I might be able to help you with your little problem. I am waiting for the arrival of two men from Chicago named Hassan and Khalik" The Mexican said with a very strong accent. "Would that be you guys?" He asked.

"Yeah man that's us. Who you say you were?" Khalik questioned as they looked at each other.

"My name is Juan Valenzuela, Jose's uncle. I want you to meet with me in two hours in the hotel restaurant and be sure to be dressed properly."

"Wait why you want us to meet you in the restaurant?" Hassan questioned.

"I have to talk to my boss, and he is who you are going to have to meet with; his name is Juan Chavez. If you are really looking for what you say you are, then this is the man to talk to. He will be expecting you." Juan walked off. As he walked away from Khalik and Hassan, Juan made a phone call. "Yeah, we got things going as planned. They are to meet with Chavez in a couple of hours. Good, then I will call you later with the rest of the details." Juan explained over the phone to Jose as he proceeded to walk away.

"Damn Hassan things keep getting better and better man. We should have gotten rid of Jimmy's ass a long time ago." Hassan said

"Didn't you say Jimmy's connect was named Chave. And Jose's uncle just said the connect name is Chavez. I wonder is it the same person; I mean it got to be because I know all these motherfuckers do not have identical names and shit."

"Yeah I guess you're right. Shit, it just keeps getting better in a superior way. We already done took this nigga for all he got, including his life, and we are still taking shit from him even after his ass is gone. Damn we're good." Hassan Said as they both began to laugh.

Juan walked into Chavez office. "Juan, to what do I owe the pleasure?" He asked

"Well, Mr. Chavez I have some very interesting people that I thought you would want to meet with."

"Uh huh, so who are these people that I am going to find interesting?"

"As I was on the beach today, I ran into the two young men whom I mentioned to you before about doing some business with. Not only are they looking for some business, but they also used to work for Jimmy Johnson in Chicago."

"They worked for Jimmy, huh; well you are right this is something very interesting. Do you know where these two are now?"

"No, but I told them to come to the restaurant in a couple of hours." Juan said.

"Yes, and make sure that you find out everything there is to know about their little history with Jimmy. I am anxious to meet these two," Said Chavez. Chavez and Jimmy had done business several times before in the past, and Jimmy was always legit with his work. There were often times when Jimmy and some of his men would spend their weekends enjoying the sandy beaches and beautiful women while Jazell and Lovely played and became good friends. Chavez trusted very few but Jimmy were one of the few that he had known for years and trusted. He had been close to his family, and Chavez would have done almost anything for him so anyone affiliated with Jimmy, he knew were legit.

Hassan and Khalik walked into the restaurant wearing some new expensive suits, looking like they were two completely different people, definitely not from the streets of Chicago.

"Yes are you gentlemen joining someone this evening?" The man asked.

"We're here to see Mr. Chavez."

"Ah yes, right this way gentleman." He escorted them to the back of the restaurant where they walked behind another area separated from the rest of the restaurant by fancy curtains. There sat Chavez, smoking a Cuban cigar, and his Mexican Mafia of twenty men all dressed in expensive tailored suits surrounded around a big marble table. "Mr. Chavez your guest has arrived."

Chavez looked at them with one eyebrow lifted pulling the cigar from his mouth dropping the ashes into a marbled ashtray. "Please join us for dinner." He extended his hand for them to sit down as the waiter pulled out the chair for them to be seated.

Khalik and Hassan held out their hands to shake the hands of a man who had more money than they had ever seen in their lives. "It's a pleasure to meet you Mr. Chavez." They both said shaking his hand, before sitting down at the table.

"My man Juan here says you two are looking for something, and you are planning to spend a substantial amount. So tell me, How much is a sizeable amount where you from?"

"A few gs or a million," Hassan said.

Chavez started to laugh as did the twenty men mafia crew at the table. "A few thousand to a million huh, well I was thinking more along the lines of fifty to a hundred million or so, but hey everyone can't be like me. Tell me why should I make you two apart of my family? It's obvious you have no real money for me to invest my time in so why should I even bother?"

"Well we worked for a well-known dealer in Chicago......"

"Ah, yes, I understand." He already knew all about them working for Jimmy, but he did not know that they were the two that killed him. "You must have loyalty in this business, loyalty to me, and respect." He raised his finger pointing to the two of them. "This is not to be confused with my money. I will do anything to anyone who tries to fuck me, friend, or family, so as long as you be loyal to me then I will be good to you." Two of Chavez's men rose up from their chairs, standing directly behind Hassan and Khalik pointing their guns at them, "But just so where all clear on things once you join this family there is only one way out. And that is to die because then you would have known far too much about me and my organization."

They looked at Chavez knowing that everything he had just said to them he meant. And everything Chavez meant he would do. This was no minor business, and if they were really going to take over Chicago then this is what they had to do. "We're clear." Hassan said.

"Good then welcome to my family, now let's eat." Chavez raised his glass in the air to make a toast. He could tell by the look in their eyes that they had never done any major dealings before, but also that they had what it took to get the job done. The same look he had in his eyes when he was out to get it, and this was even more reason for him to keep his eyes on his new runners. "To the fresh additions to this family, we welcome you."

"Yes welcome." The woman said walking in with a glass of Champaign and a younger woman following behind her.

"Gentlemen this is my good-looking wife Maria Chavez and our beautiful daughter Jazell Chavez." Jazell was her name, but everyone called her Zell. Her skin was caramel with long silky brown hair draping down her shoulders. Her eyes were big with a hue of chestnut, lips' pouty, succulent, and full with lengthy legs, wide hips, and the perfect body. She looked like a goddess.

"Oh yes, one more thing," Chavez said, "No one is to lay a hand on my daughter, or they will have to answer to me, and if you have to answer to me then you will be no longer living to answer to anyone else."

Hassan and Khalik looked at the monstrous look in his eyes. His daughter, his only daughter is the most precious to him and if anyone had crossed that path, there would be hell to pay.

"Daddy, stop it." Jazell said to her father kissing him on the cheek.

"Hello" They both said kissing the two women on the back of their hands.

"It's a pleasure to meet you." Hassan said looking Zell deep in her eyes. They had an instant connection between them, but he knew that he could never be with someone like her. She was the boss's daughter and mixing business with pleasure was not at any time a good thing, especially if he wanted to stay alive.

Hassan stood on the balcony of the presidential suit overlooking the beach sipping on a glass of a $5,000 bottle Courvoisier L'Esprit Decanter, wearing a black silk Versace robe. The same robe he had made Jimmy take off and give to him right before he killed him. He stepped back in off the balcony and headed into the bathroom to take a shower when he heard a knock at the door. He opened the door and there was the housekeeper standing there. "Yeah did you need something?" Hassan asked the housekeeper.

"Yes sir I was just bringing in the fresh towels you requested."

"Thanks, put them down over on the table."

"Yes." The housekeeper placed the towels on the table and exited the room. Hassan closed the door and went into the bathroom to take his shower.

The front door to his suite opened up. *Here we go girl pull yourself together cause there's no going back.* Jazell walked in noticing that the music was playing in the bedroom. She walked in seeing that Hassan was in the shower.

Damn that water felt good. He thought, stepping out of the hot steaming water, cutting the shower off. He dried off the dripping water trickling from his body, walking naked into the bedroom in all of his fineness.

"I hope I'm not interrupting anything."

Hassan looked up dropping his towel to the floor startled by her presence. "How did you get in here? What the hell are you doing?"

"You really should start locking the door behind you."

"Your father will kill me if he finds you in here."

"You let me worry about my father." Jazell said.

"Don't be sneaking up on me like that." He placed the all-black silk robe back on after drying off. "Aint nothing like Versace," Black was his color; he was a dark chocolate black man with the smoothest skin a brother could have.

"Oh yeah baby you're wearing it real well." Jazell said trying to stroke his ego.

Hassan pulled out a small sack of cocaine and poured a tiny amount onto the dresser, lining it up with a sharp razor blade. He took a 100-dollar bill out of his wallet and rolled it up snorting two lines. Hassan was already high. The two lines made him feel as if he was floating on a cloud.

"So you're gonna let me get a little of that?" Jazell asked walking behind him putting her hands around his waist grabbing his dick. She walked around in front of him bending over to snort a line of the cocaine.

"No, what are you doing." Hassan said with an instant bulge peeping from out of the robe. "Give me that," He grabbed the 100-dollar bill out of her hand after she snorted some of the cocaine. "Look, you need to go."

"You wouldn't want me to tell my father how bad you've been treating me would you?" she turned around staring Hassan directly in his face so close that he could kiss her. *I don't think he would appreciate* what I have to say, and he does have a bad temper. Besides it looks like somebody got a little excited to see me." She pushed him onto the bed. "I'm not making you feel uncomfortable am I?" Whispering into his ear straddled over him.

"You're not making me uncomfortable; you're good" Hassan placed his hand on her face looking into her eyes. "I don't want you to leave, but like I said I don't want your father to find out about you being here," Kissing her on the forehead.

"I don't want to go" Jazell looked into his eyes before she kissed him.

Hassan looked back at Jazell, knowing now that she was feeling him like he was feeling her. "You don't have to go anywhere baby" kissing her passionately.

Jazell pulled her hair out of the ponytail letting it drape down her shoulders, then slowly began taking off her clothes leaving on her panty, and bra set that was covered in black see through lace.

Damn this girl is beautiful. Hassan thought to himself kicking off his shoes.

Jazell climbed back onto the bed straddling on top of him kissing him on his neck. She began taking off his shirt while kissing slowly down his chest.

"You are so beautiful," Hassan told Jazell rubbing on her booty. He unsnapped the bra, taking it off her. Her breasts were so firm. He grabbed them with both of his hands sucking and nibbling on her nipples while she held his head closer to her breast. Hassan laid her down and got off the bed pulling down his pants and boxers.

Damn, he is big. She thought to herself.

Hassan started pulling off Jazell's panties mesmerized with how pretty her pussy was; shaved, smooth, and bald. *Her pussy is fat; he* thought as he placed two fingers inside of her. He watched as they went in and out while she became more and more wet each time.

She moaned "Oh that feels so good." As she layback on the bed with her eyes closed, he places his tongue on her clit slowly stroking up, down, and in a circular motion all around the walls of her vagina. Still fingering her with now three fingers, Jazell's legs start to shake. He pulls his fingers out of her and licks her juices from them; climbing into the bed on top of her, spreading her legs open, so he could get between them. His manhood was rock hard, and he wanted to feel her so bad, but he did not want to hurt her. Slowly, he inserted his self inside, feeling all the wetness that she had, stroking in and out, as he placed her legs on top of his shoulders. "Yeah" he moaned softly in her ear.

Jazell began to moan even louder as he pounded inside of her. She felt every inch of him, and she liked it. Hassan let her legs down and climbed from on top of her. He lay on the bed as she climbed back on top, mounting upon him backwards, riding his manhood.

Ooh, what is she doing? Hassan had never had a woman ride him backwards before or even take control over him in the bedroom. He was fire, and his lovemaking drove the woman crazy. Jazell rode him then she placed her legs further apart, bending her body forward with her hands down in front of her between his legs. She bounced on him even harder. "Oh shit!" Hassan yelled out loudly not even realizing the noise he was making. They both began to moan louder and louder as she rode him from the back. With each thrust, the sex became more intense.

Her legs were shaking, and he grabbed her ass slapping it and making it bounce even harder. "I about to cum" Jazell said making Hassan grip her ass tighter.

"Cum for me boo, cum on this hard ass dick"

"Oh yes baby" she came trembling and shaking all through her body.

"I'm about to cum, oh shit get up." Jazell hopped off Hassan grabbing his manhood, stroking him; letting all of his cum squirt all in her hands.

"Damn" They both said lying on the bed before Jazell realized her hands was full of cum. She got up and went into the bathroom to wash up. As she walked back into the room, she laid next to Hassan in the bed were they cuddled up and fell asleep in each other's arms.

"Good morning sleepy head." Jazell said as Hassan opened his eyes in disbelief that she was with him last night.

He still wanted to get with her even though he knew if her father found out he would be in serious trouble, but he did not care at all. Jazell was beautiful. She had this type of beauty that made you get lost just looking at her. "Good morning." He said.

There was a knock on the door. "Damn, who in the hell is that?" Hassan said as the knocking got louder.

"I got to get the door, get in the closet." He opened the door for her to hide into the closet. "Stay right there, I'll be back." He walked out of the room and answered the front door.

"What's up?" It was Khalik.

"What's up?" He said, "You here early nigga."

"So, get your ass up. Let me get something to drink you want some?"

"Yeah let me get some of that." They walked over to the dining area where all the drinks were at the bar. "I could get used to this type of life man." Khalik said.

"You know what, I almost forgot, I got to take a shower. I'll meet you in a minute," Rushing Khalik out of the room.

"Oh yeah," He looked around the room, "Nigga, who you got up in here?"

Hassan walked him into the foyer leading through the living room "Man, I think I fucked up. I got Mr. Chavez's daughter up in the room."

"What! Come on man, what are you doing? Get her the fuck out of here before somebody finds out she was in this motherfucker. Damn man you gonna get us killed."

Khalik shook his head to the words flowing from Hassan's lips, telling him something he really was not expecting to hear. They were in Mexico and the one thing they had to do other than prove their loyalty and trust to Chavez was to stay away from his daughter, but already that rule had been broken. Hassan had fucked up, and they needed to make sure no one found out about this, or they were never going to make it home. They needed to focus, and he needed to get his head out of the clouds and back in gear.

Chapter Eight
The Lovely Plan

Lovely thought about everything she was planning and how it was starting to come together just as she had envisioned it to. She had found out that Khalik, Hassan had killed uncles Jimmy by setting him up, and using her for their own sick pleasures in the process; but her revenge shall be much sweeter. She had the both of them eating all the trash thrown out to them and meanwhile, Khalik's only pride and joy, his brother Tre, would be the first to get finished off as a bonus. Her pleasure was to see them pay, but not until she collects what is due to her; and all that they have earned in the process. Oh *how nice it is, the taste of sweet revenge.* She smiled evilly to herself.

Lovely thought about making her plot for revenge, she knew that Khalik and Hassan had been trying to get this kind of hustle on for quite some time now, and she knew they had what it took to do the shit. After hearing about her Uncle Jimmy's death and to find out those were the guys who murdered him was a lot to take in. They were people whom she had known for a while and never once did it come up that they were selling dope for Jimmy. She felt like they used her to get their own sick pleasures while plotting to set him up.

Lovely made a deal with Detective's Whitman and Smith to get rid of them, they hated blacks and to make a deal with her; she knew that they would do anything to get them off the streets. Meanwhile, she had plotted to get close to Khalik's brother Tre to see if he knew anything about the money, they took from the safe. Lovely knew that her uncle had always kept at least a few thousand to a million dollars in that safe, but she knew that there was much more where that came from, she just did not know where he kept the rest. She had her eyes on them.

Every step they took she was watching, and it was just a matter of time before she got everything. Her plan was to see them rise to the top before destroying and leaving them penny less and buried six feet deep. *If Khalik and Hassan only knew that at any time, they could be dead.* She thought to herself. Lovely continued thinking of what she should do and how she would do it. *I just need some time that's it, keep your head in the game Lov.*

Driving in a drop top candy red 66' Cadillac Coup Deville sitting on gold 23-inch rims and listening to The Chronic album, Tre pulls up to The Halstead National Bank over on north Halstead Street where he worked. He steps out with a clean-cut and shaved to match his high self-confidence and good looks. Tre straightened his tie and posture as he walked into the bank when he noticed this female. She was fine, about 5'3 with long dark-brown hair that had light brown highlights, and she was dressed in Chanel from her shades right down to her feet and the briefcase she held close to her side. Tre knew she could not have lived around here because he grew up in Englewood and knew just about everybody in and around all the surrounding areas.

She walked over to the counter for one of the associates to help her, as she waited in line, when she noticed Tre. She walked over towards him switching in her white denim Chanel jeans and smoky grey blouse hanging over one shoulder, sporting an oversized grey and silver bag with white and silver stilettos. "Hi, are you free to help me for a second?" She said reaching out her hand to shake Tre's hand.

"Yes," He knew he had to hurry up and find out who she was. "Thank you for waiting. My name is Treshon Givens; I am an accountant here at Halstead." He reached out to shake her hand. "Your name is?"

"Janae Luvell." She reached out to shake Tre's hand once more.

There was a diamond on her finger that looked like it could stop traffic, it was huge.

"What is it that I can do for you?" Tre asked politely in his most professional voice.

Janae rose up from the seat. "I am new to town, and I would like to open an account here."

"Well first I would have to establish a few things, so how about we go back over to my desk." Tre followed behind her as she headed to his desk. "Have a seat." He said pulling out the chair for her to be seated. "So where are you from and how long have you been here in town?"

"Well, I have a relative who lives here who told me to come and check things out to try to get away from back home for a while, you know, a change of scenery."

"Oh, well where are you staying?"

"Umm I'm staying over on East Walton Place at the Drake Hotel."

Tre paused for a minute looking blank. "Why would you want to bank here if you are staying in a place like that? No offence but it is pretty pricey."

"I saw this bank first as I was passing through so I decided to come here." She said giving Tre any answer to stop him from questioning her.

"Well what kind of account would you like to open, a checking account?"

"No, a high interest account is what I'm going to need. I'm depositing a large amount of money."

"I'm going to need your picture ID." She handed him the documents from her purse and answered any questions he proceeded to ask while she filled out and signed the proper paperwork needed to open the account. Along the way Tre explained to her all the information she needed to know about the account. "Now all you have to do at the moment is put in the minimum balance for this account to stay open and active."

Janae reached down beside her and grabbed the briefcase from off of the floor. She opened it and looked inside, then handed the briefcase to Tre. Inside was a large sum of money. "That's the amount I would like to deposit. It should be about 50 thousand in there."

Tre looked up at Janae "This is a lot of money to be carrying around in your bag. Do you work around here?" Wondering where she got the money from with no job. "Normally we can't take a large amount over 10 thousand dollars without the IRS being involved. So are you sure you want to place that much in your account?"

"Umm, well, no I don't work around here I just closed my business back home, and these are all of my savings and profits. I need this money put up, because otherwise I may get robbed or something carrying it in my purse like this." She smiled

"I guess I can see what I can do for you. Well, we will just finish up with the process, and I will take care of it for you. I know a few tricks to handle things like this." Tre finished up with the account information then handed her a receipt for the deposit. "Thank you Mr....."

"Givens, Treshon Givens."

"Yes, Mr. Treshon," Acting as if she had forgotten his name already. "Thanks for all your help." She stood up from the chair gathering all the paperwork from the table.

"You're very welcome Ms. Luvell." He said grinning.

She began walking away. "Lovely, call me lovely." Looking back at Tre and winking. She stepped outside making a phone call as she got into her car.

"Ok we're all set on this end, just be you, sexy, flirty, and about that money. The nigga is easy as gold and all you have to do is put it to him, one good time, and he's all yours, shit no man can stand to turn down the power of the pussy, and you know that shit is lethal." She said jokingly,

"Your gonna go to the Cabrini's, and you know what to do from there." *Yeah, I got something for their asses.* Lovely thought as she hung the phone up preparing herself for the ultimate deception, getting into her pink 92' Lexus SC400, which was only one of her cars, with mirrored window tint and silver 18-inch rims shining as she drove off.

Tre pulled up to Cabrini Green when he notices this fine young female standing out in front of the building. It was 12:30 in the afternoon, and the hustlers was out with their candy-colored cars and drop tops while the basketball court was swarming with brothers sporting wife beaters, basketball shorts, and fresh pairs of sneaks. It seemed like it's constantly something going on around there and was always full of people, mostly a lot of wanna be dealers and their two-bit ass friends trying to hustle these fools out of their money.

"Hey ma what's up?" Tre walked up to the building, "How you doing? I just wanted to introduce myself to you. I saw you sitting up here looking all nice, and I was wondering if you had a man?"

"No I'm single," looking as if she was all of that "what about you?"

"I'm single too. My name is Treshon, by the way, but my peeps call me Tre"

"I'm Nyla"

"That's a pretty name'" Tre commented, "So Nyla, can I get your number where I can call you sometime?"

"Yeah, but I have an even better idea, why don't we just get the hell out of here and go somewhere where we can get more acquainted." Nyla told Tre whispering in his ear. "Meet me over at the Marriot around the street over on Halsted in about an hour, in room 215." Even though Nyla was going along with the plan to get closer to Tre to find out where Khalik and Hassan had hidden the money, she always enjoyed the company of a good-looking man. For her, this was more about pleasure than helping her best friend.

"Alright, wait, what are you doing over here any ways?'""

"I was just visiting someone, a girlfriend of mines."

"Oh yeah who," Tre asked

"Well, apparently I had the wrong apartments, so I was just leaving when you came up. You see I'm from the east side so you know, I barely come this way. Any ways, are you going to take me up on that offer or are we gonna sit and chat all day?"

"Yeah, give me a minute, and I'll be there." He watched as Nyla walked off, looking at her ass. "Damn!"

Nyla got into her car and pulled off, calling lovely on the phone. "Yeah, so I did what you asked, he's gonna meet me in 20 minutes at a hotel, so I will keep you posted." She hung the phone up.

Tre got out of the car and headed up the stairs to the back of the hotel to room 215. He knocked on the door.

"It's open, come on in." Nyla yelled out from behind the other side of the door as she had the door slightly cracked ajar for him to enter.

Tre walked in, "Hey. What's up? It's Tre, where you at?"

"Yeah, here I come now" Nyla came from the bathroom wearing nothing walking towards Tre. His eyes got big, *damn*. He thought quietly to himself. Nyla approached him. She was tall and dark skinned with a nice figure. Her nipples were erect, sticking straight out from her breast, round and firm looking. You could tell that she worked on her physique because she had a washboard stomach with a firm backside. She was beautiful, and she knew it.

Nyla walked in the front of Tre where she stood whispering in his ear "Do you like what you see?" She asked grabbing his hands and placing them on her ass.

"Hell yeah" Tre said.

Nyla bent down and unbuckled his belt, he was hard as a rock, and she could tell from the bulge that was in his pants. She pulled them down along with his boxers letting his manhood stare her straight in the face. *Oh yeah he is packing something large. She* thought. Nyla placed her tongue on his manhood and began to lick circles around the head. Then she started to suck with a tight grip in her jaws.

"Oh shit girl where you learn to suck dick like that, damn" He moaned and grunted as if it was his first time in years, and he was finally getting to feel the pleasures of a woman again. He grabbed Nyla and pulled her up turning her towards the bed. "Bend that ass over" taking his manhood and forcing it in. She was wide, open, and wet as hell, he knew for damn sure she was not a virgin. Nyla started to moan as he thrust his self inside of her deeper, and it felt greater each time, causing her to moan even louder.

"Ooh, yeah Tre, fuck that good pussy. I knew you wanted this just as bad as I wanted you" Nyla started to throw it back to Tre bouncing her ass up and down as he went in and out of her. The grunts and moans became louder and more intense as the sweat rolled down their bodies. "Oh yeah daddy work this pussy and make me come."

Tre became even more turned on by the sound of her voice. As he thrust inside of her harder and harder, she threw back more forcefully. "Cum for me bitch" He said, pulling her hair and slapping her ass.

Nyla was getting weak in the knees. She loved it when a man talked to her like that during sex. "Fuck me harder, pull my hair harder, talk to me" He did exactly what she was asking for. "I'm cumin Tre; I'm cumin" Her body began to tremble, and Tre started to feel her moistness.

"Shit!" he yelled out "Damn, this pussy good. I'm about to cum" Tre grabbed Nyla's shoulders and started to pump even harder causing Nyla to scream some more. "Oh yeah" He came, pulling out of her as the cum dripped out and trickled down her leg. Neither one of them caring that he had just cum inside of her. Tired from the sex, they both laid on the bed naked as they passed out.

Chapter Nine

Prison Break

"**H**ey, Youngster, what you stressing bout," Keeper said waking Khalik up from his daydream. Shit you ought to be happy you about to get out of this motherfucker. Anyway, youngster, they opened the doors, so I'm gonna hit the TV room, you coming?"

"Yeah man, I need to get out of this cell for a minute." Khalik said rising from the uncomfortable cot, he was laying on. They walked out of the cell and went into the TV room where the news was on and every nigga in the room was surrounding the TV.

"What the hell going on over here? What's up, fuck is going on?" Keeper said as him and Khalik approached the crowd of inmates surrounding around the TV.

"Shit, man it was a big bust. They got about 20 of them boys out there." Said another inmate

"Who? What up?" Khalik questioned trying to figure out what went on and what everybody was so excited about. In prison, everything was a big deal since all they did was stay locked up all day long with nowhere to go but up in another nigga face every corner they turned.

"Yeah man they killed bout' 20 of them boys out there. Monteco and his crewmember. These niggas dropping like flies. You know them boys young. They weren't gonna last no way, robbing motherfuckers and shit." The inmate continued.

Monteco was a youngster that came up with Khalik and Hassan. He started his own little crew selling drugs too, only they were more into robbing and doing the drugs rather than selling them and stacking their paper. Monteco was always crazy. Khalik remembered several times when he did stupid things and was surprised; he had not been killed sooner. This made him think about after Jimmy was killed how things started getting better but then got worse by the second. Soon Khalik would find out that Jimmy had a brother who was locked up, and no one knew about him. If they did, they never talked about him.

Illinois State Prison, Jamel Johnson sat on the edge of the cot in his cell in a conversation with his cellmate and another inmate.

"Shit, they say that nigga Jimmy Johnson just got sprayed, dead." One of the inmates yelled out walking through the hall, passing Jamel's cell.

"Damn, that's fucked-up man," Said another with a sense of sorrow in his voice as if he knew him personally.

Jamel rose up; he could not believe his ears. "Jimmy Johnson?" He asked as he walked out the cell towards the inmate spreading the news.

"Yeah man, I just heard it on the news."

"Hell naw, you don't know what the hell you talking 'bout" Jamel said to the inmate getting angry at what he thought was pure bullshit. *This young motherfucker trying to get some attention*, He thought. *These niggas has to be lying, they always saying some stupid shit.*

"For real man I just came from the TV room where I heard it."

Jamel walked down to the TV room and rushed through to the front of the crowd.

"Here it goes. It's coming on again, turn that shit up man." An inmate said.

As he stood there listening to the reporter, Jamel could not believe what he was hearing.

Late last night, long time drug lord Jimmy Johnson was found murdered in his 300,000 dollar home in the Gold Coast area of Chicago. He had been shot several times, including a shot in the head and robbed for what appears to be drugs, both marijuana and cocaine, and very large amounts of it. Police think that it may have been someone or multiple people who may have known Jimmy well, but so far, no arrest has been made. Police are, however, investigating this. From channel 10 news, I am Barbara Wells.

Jamel could not believe what he was hearing. *Jimmy, dead,* He turned around walking away from the TV in disbelief. He wanted to feel sad that Jimmy had been killed, and in some ways, he did, but he could not help but to feel this instant anger and rage. This had only deepened the wound from some of the pain he had endured over the years. In fact, he had encountered a new painfulness in his heart, a numbness that had never been there before.

He wanted them dead. He wanted to kill them, his self, and he would have if only he was out in the world to do so. This was his own flesh and blood, which he hated for being able to be free but loved with all the passion in his heart. Someone betrayed his brother and taken his life. Someone killed Jimmy, but whom?

As he rests his head upon his hands lying on the pillow, Jamel began to think of a quick plan to escape the prison. He would not need any help. Someone else would just slow him down and create more problems for him. This was something that had to be done by him and only him. His thoughts were racing through his mind, traveling a million miles a second. He could not help but to think about the vicious things that went on in that house, how they probably tortured him before they killed him. Whoever did this was going to pay and Jamel would make sure of it.

Jamel closed his eyes and prayed. *Dear Lord, for all the wrong I have done. Nothing is going to amount to the pain I am about to conflict on these fools. I hope you can forgive me someday, if not, I shall burn in hell for my sins.*

As the weeks went by Khalik, and Hassan had been pushing large amounts of cocaine and a little heroin from time to time. Since they had taken the trip to Mexico and met up with Chavez, things were looking good for them. Jose was the one who convinced him that he; Khalik, and Hassan had what it took to take over the streets of Chicago. Despite Jose's presence, they had mentioned to Chavez that they were some of the most loyal people he would know, and that he could trust them with everything he had, even his life.

From that point on, they were in there, and they had been making more money than they could have ever imagined, far more than they were getting from robbing people for their belongings. Meanwhile, Jose was in and out because of his grandmother's passing and then several more problems going on in his family, while they quickly begin to earn a name for themselves.

Things had gotten so bad with his family that whenever he did get out there he had a problem snorting more than he was selling. Jose was really close to his grandmother and her dying hit him hard. Jose started developing a habit with cocaine, which made him act stupid and out of control, becoming someone whom they did not recognize. While Khalik and Hassan were getting richer, Jose felt as if he was being left out and forgotten about.

That would soon change. Jose would subsequently show and prove that if it were not for him, then they would not be running things. He started to feel remorse and anger; feeling as though they would both pay for leaving him stuck out when it all happened through him. He felt as if they owed it to him to cut him in on any deal they cashed in on, but they were not.

"Hey Smith, we got your favorite street man here, picked up again for another one of his episodes." The officer yelled out through the precinct to Detective Smith as he brought Jose in with his hands cuffed behind his back yelling and cursing the officer. "Hey! Calm down." The officer told Jose. "Yeah, we picked him up for running a red light and swerving on the road. He almost got his self in an accident. Oh, yeah we found a little cocaine stashed on him. He's high now."

"Well, well, if it isn't my main man Jose Valenzuela." Smith began to mock from what he thought to be street language. "You know Jose I have been looking for you, and you're a hard man to find for someone who's always in the streets. I see you can't seem to stay away for very long," Smirking at Jose.

"Fuck you man." Jose looked up at Smith, wishing he could take the handcuffs off and punch him in his face.

"You know Jose it's very ironic that you came to visit us today, because you see, I have been working on a case that I can't seem to get a break with, an assault case." Detective Smith shuffled through the files laid upon his desk and stopped when he came to the case, he had mentioned to Jose. "Here, why don't you pull up a seat; let me have a talk with you for a moment." He said as he pointed to the chair in front of him on the other side of the desk.

"I don't need to sit down. I'm good; just take these cuffs off of me." Jose said with his hands squirming behind his back.

"Sit down ass hole." The officer said placing him in the seat.

"Any ways, what's that got to do with me?" Jose responded to Smith's insinuation that he had something to do with the assault.

"Well, you see; the case is about Khalik Givens and Hassan Waters, and I know that you run with these two from time to time. I also know that Khalik, and you were like family at some point. Word on the streets is that these two are selling drugs around here and from the looks of it, it seems as though they might be leaving you out. I know this happens to be true because I've had my eyes on you and them."

"You don't know what you talking 'bout." Jose frowned up at Smith, turning his head in the other direction.

"Maybe not, but what I do have is several tips that say you might have something to do with it. The only problem is, is that I cannot seem to get any of them to come down and write a statement. Not to mention I just don't have all the evidence I need to put you ass holes away for good." Smith said, bluffing his words, knowing that he was the one who had been responsible for Jimmy's death, and he knew almost about everything that went down on the streets because he was on almost everyone's payroll.

"Therefore, I have nothing. You seem to forget that I know about that little robbery that took place a few years back with that young kid who was minding his own business and just happened to be robbed by some punks who looked exactly like you guys. If it hadn't been for some connections with your friends late connect Jimmy, you guys would've been sitting in jail." Smith seemed to get angrier by the minute.

"Look at me, you bastard." Smith began to tap his pen on the desk eyeballing Jose. "You know what pisses me off about this? It's that you motherfuckers think you can get passed me with everything."

"Man look, I don't know anything 'bout that shit you talking. Word is bond." Jose said glancing over at Smith then turning his head away again.

"Oh, well I suppose you know more than I do so why don't we make us a little deal where we both get what we want." Jose turned back around. Smith had peaked an interest and had gotten his attention. Smith looked Jose in his eyes as Jose looked up at him. He could tell he had gotten under his skin with the statement he just made, and he knew if the price was right that Jose would do anything to get what he wanted because Jose only cared about Jose.

Jose sat and stared into the eyes of his enemy, the law, who had never been on his side and at no time would they be. *Snake ass law.* He thought. Smith looked back at Jose as if he could hear what he was thinking. He gave the look that he had all the answers to his problems and all he had to do is get Jose to play by his game, but it would be a treacherous game to play. No rules, just strategy, and fearlessness.

The game in which no one from the streets wanted to lose and anyone who dared to play could be caught in the crossfire. It would be the battle of the strongest in the fight for who would be king in the streets, the realest motherfucker, or the law. No matter, the consequences, no matter the risk, life or death and any man for his self.

11:00 a.m. Jamel worked in the prison chow hall as he did every day during lunch on the serving line. He began to lean over a bit as if he was not feeling well, when another inmate noticed and took his place on the line.

"Hey man, you look sick. Look here, I'll serve, and you go in the back and get yourself together so these motherfuckers won't have anything to mess with us about."

"Aiight, thanks, good looking out man." Jamel said to the inmate. He walked off the line and headed towards the back.

"Hey, what's going on over there?" One of the guards yelled out.

"Nothing. Everything is good."The same inmate responded.

It was one of the slowest times of the day, and Jamel knew that this was the correct time for the escape to occur. This is when it would be less surveillance watching over certain locations within the prison like the area where the maintenance is done, which was right next to the chow hall. As he quickly walked into the back without anyone paying too much attention, Jamel hid into one of the maintenance rooms when the civilian maintenance supervisor turned his back. He waited a few minutes until the supervisor left the hall. As he was leaving, the guard working the floor walked towards the maintenance room where Jamel was hiding after hearing a whistling noise coming from that way.

As the guard approached the room door, he opened it but seen nothing but supplies in a dark room. He walked in placing one hand on his gun that rests in his holster. The guard continued to walk further into the room but saw or heard nothing when Jamel came from behind him. He grabbed the gun with one hand while placing his other hand over the guard's mouth.

"Now, I'm gonna take my hand off, and if you make one sound I will kill your ass." Jamel said to the young guard who was scared and had only been working there a few short weeks. He removed his hands from the guards' mouth. "Now turn around and get undressed."

"Oh my God are you going to rape me? Please man don't do it, I'll do whatever you say man." The guard pleaded.

"Do I look like a bitch to you motherfucker, huh?" Jamel got angry. He wanted to show him just how bitch a man could be after getting the shit whooped out of him, but he had no time for that. He needed to move quickly, and the guard was wasting his time, so he took the back end of the gun and cold cocked him in the head, knocking him out completely.

Once the guard was subdued, Jamel begins to remove some of his clothes and put them on. Luckily, the guard was just about the right size. After he removed his clothes, Jamel took the shirt that he wore and ripped it, tying the guard up. Once he tied him up, he placed another piece of the ripped shirt into his mouth and gagged, then hid him in a closet full of supplies. Jamel searched the pockets of the clothing where he found a wallet that contained the guard's credit cards and identification.

He picked the hat up from the floor and placed it on his head, walking out of the room, making sure that no one was near the hall. Then he began to walk away with his hat slightly covering the sight of his eyes and his head looking more towards the ground. This way, no one could look at him straight in the eyes and recognize who he was before escaping the prison. Jamel finally got close to the entranceway of the prison.

"Going home for the day?" the guard at the desk asked.

"Yeah, leaving a little early today, I'll see you guys tomorrow." He said glancing at the man and quickly turning back so he would not be recognized.

"O.k. see you tomorrow." The guard replied.

Jamel had made it to the front entrance and passed everyone in the prison, all he needed to do is get through the gate, and he was home free. The guard buzzed him out of the gated area coming from the back. Jamel walked through and stepped out of the front door. He began to walk fast, but not too fast, where it would draw suspicion. As he continued to walk further out, he noticed the prison maintenance pickup truck, so he walked towards it and waited until the men were in the building. They left the back of the truck opened so Jamel sneaked his way in and hid in the back of the truck behind several boxes. The men eventually made their way back to the truck and locked up and Jamel had made his escape from the prison grounds.

Chapter Ten
Double Dose

Nyla lay on the couch watching T.V. Her eyes were dazed as she started to feel nauseous from the soda; she had just drunk a little while ago. *Damn why can't I get rid of this flu, what's wrong with me?* She asked herself looking as if she was extremely ill. *Come on snap out of it girl, we have to get back on track and get back to work for lovely's ass start tripping.* She thought as she rose from off of the couch. Nyla walked into the kitchen, *what could I eat to take care of an upset stomach? Maybe some crackers or toast will help.* She fixed her some toast then spread peanut butter on top and quickly ate it. *Oh, god that made me feel a whole lot better.*

It was almost nine o'clock on a Sunday, and she knew that she would have to get up early if she wanted to get to her appointment on time. She decided to take a shower and go to bed a little as soon as possible so she could rest and get up in time.

The next morning she got up and got ready for her appointment, "Alright let me grab my purse and head out." She spoke loudly to herself, when her cell phone rang. It was Lovely.

"Hello"

"Where the fuck have you been huh, I've been calling you the last couple of days and got no answer or a call back? Have you spoken to Tre at all lately?" Lovely raised her voice to Nyla.

"Yeah Lovely I have been kicking it with him a few times, but he's not trying to say anything, so I really don't think he knows anything. Why don't you just go talk with his brother and confront his ass about what it is you know, shit all this for some dough? You got plenty of that." Nyla tried to convince her.

"Hold up bitch, first off, it's not just some dough; it's my uncles dough, which means it's my dough that they stole, and any ways I thought you were my girl why you fronting on me like you don't want to help me out, besides it's been a month almost now, and you should know something. Khalik and Hassan, it's hard, but I got them under my eye, but if you can find something out from him, then why not. I mean you get to have a little dick in the process any ways." Lovely explained.

"The nigga is fine as hell."

"Uh, yeah, that's why I need you to be on your p's and q's."

"Look I'm sorry. I just haven't been feeling myself lately that's all. Any ways I got an appointment to get to, and I'll call you later." Nyla said rushing her off the phone.

"Yeah, alright, make sure you do that, bye." Lovely said hanging up the phone.

Nyla pulled up to the St Bernard Hospital on W. 64th Street. She pulled into the parking garage and found a space then got out of her 1992 black Jaguar. She walked into the elevator through the parking garage and went to the fourth floor of the hospital. *Dr. Kent* she thought looking on the hospital map. *Take a left and go straight to the end of the hall, all right then.* As she walked down the hall, she came to the door of the doctor whom she was going to see. "Yes, I have a ten o'clock appointment with Dr. Kent"

"Alright, sign your name and have a seat and someone will be with you shortly." The nurse replied with a smile on her face pretending that she liked sitting at that desk all day long.

"O.k., thanks" Ten minutes had passed by as Nyla wondered what was taking so long one of the nurses called her name.

"Nyla Carrolton"

"Yes, that's me" Nyla rose up from her seat and headed to the back with the nurse.

"O.k. step on the scale and let me get your weight" She stepped on the scale.

"144 is what you weigh, you can step down, and take a seat right here and let me take your vitals."

How did I gain six pounds in a few weeks when I cannot seem to keep anything down? Nyla began thinking to herself as the nurse finished taking her blood pressure. "Now all I need is some blood from you, and that's it." The nurse drew blood from Nyla's arm. "All done, now if you wait in room three the doctor will be with you as soon as possible." She said walking out of the room and closing the door behind her.

A few minutes went by and there was a knock on the door, when a tall slim white man with brunette hair and light brown eyes wearing a doctor's coat walked in. "Hi, I'm Dr. Kent. What can I do for you today Ms. Carrolton?"

She looked up at the doctor "Well, I have been having problems keeping down food, and I think I may have a stomach virus or the flu coming on, or something."

"Alright, when was your last pap-smear?"

"Two months ago in April."

"O.k. when was your last menstrual period?" Dr. Kent said as he wrote on his clipboard.

"May twelfth"

"What I'm going to do is bring back a nurse with me, and we'll do a pelvic exam to see what's going on, as well as a pregnancy test. I want you to go ahead and go into the bathroom over there and pee in the cup for me afterwards set it in the window right above the cups. When you're done then come back into the room and get undressed from the waist down and lie on the table, and we will be in shortly." Dr. Kent walked out of the room with Nyla right behind him going into the bathroom and shutting the door.

Nyla read the directions on the cup. *Wipe yourself first using the cleansing napkin then place the cup under your vagina while standing over the toilet and proceed to urinate into the cup making sure to fill to the pink line.*

Shit, I hope I do not get this pee all over me. She thought, as she finished and pulled up her clothes. She placed the cup in the window and washed her hands. When she was done, she headed back into the room, got undressed below the waist, and lay on the table with a baby blue sheet covering her as she waited for the doctor and nurse.

A knock at the door, "Are you ready to go?" the nurse said walking in the room without waiting for Nyla to respond to the knock first.

"Yeah, I'm ready"

"I need you to scoot down to the very edge of the table as much as you can until your bottom reaches the edge, and then I want you to place your legs into the stirrups and spread your knees as far apart as you can get them." The nurse placed everything out on the counter whom the doctor would need for the pelvic exam.

Dr. Kent walked in and began putting on gloves and a mask. "You're not nervous are you?" Nyla shook her head yes. She hated getting these things done.

"Don't be this won't take but a few minutes." He grabbed the metal instrument from the nurse.

"This will be a bit uncomfortable, but I want you to relax." He said sliding the cold metal into her vagina.

"I am also going to check you for any infections and sexually transmitted diseases." After he finished he took out the metal instrument placing two fingers inside of her pressing on her stomach.

"Well that's it. You can get up and get yourself cleaned up, and I will be back with the results in a few. It takes about ten minutes for them to be complete, and your blood test won't be ready for a couple of days."

As the doctor and nurse walked out Nyla cleaned herself up with the wipes, the nurse gave her and put her clothes back on. *Let me wash my hands.* She thought washing her hands in the sink to get off the excess gel from when she wiped her vagina. Nyla sat in the chair next to the table she had her exam on waiting for the doctor.

Twelve minutes had passed, and the doctor walked in closing the door behind him "Well good news Ms. Carrolton; you're pregnant, about three in a half weeks along."

Nyla looked at Dr. Kent with surprise. "Oh my god, what, are you sure?"

"Yes, I'm sure and your other tests came back negative. I am going to write you a prescription for some prenatal vitamins and iron pills. Nurse Sarah is going to give you a bag with a sample bottle of vitamins, iron pills, and some pamphlets and coupons for you to read and use. I want to see you in about another month to make sure you are doing all right, so stop by the front desk and the receptionist will give you an appointment date. Did you have any questions for me?"

"No thank you." Nyla got the bag from the nurse and stopped at the front desk for her next appointment as she walked out of the doctor's office. *What am I going to do with a baby? This is so crazy right now; I cannot even believe it.* Nyla walked into the parking garage as she got into her car, she drove off still in awe about the news she had just received. She waited at the light *oh my god, three in a half weeks; that's when I started sleeping with Tre, exactly, oh no, this can't be right. Shit, this is not happening to me.*

A horn honked at Nyla as she sat at the green light thinking to herself. She looked up and realized she was holding up traffic when the horns of the people in the cars behind her began to honk. The only person who she had been with around that time was Tre. She thought to herself becoming even angrier as she thought about it. *Damn, how could I be so goddamn stupid?*

As she pieced things together in her mind, she realized that her best friend Lovely, whom she had been trying to help get information on the niggas that killed her uncle and took his money, could never know about this baby.

How would I tell him? Should I tell him? She became extremely exhausted mentally, not knowing if telling Tre would be the right thing to do especially since she hadn't thought if she would keep it or not. *I have to keep this baby.* She thought. *It's my first child and who knows if the chance to get married will ever happen. This is my baby and no matter what the consequences are, I am keeping it. Fuck him, Lovely, and everyone else. This is my life.*

As she continued to think about the last few days since she went to the doctor, Nyla sat on the couch looking out the window when the phone rang, she answered "Hello".

"Hello is this Nyla Carrolton?"

"Yes this is her, who is this?"

"This is Amber from Dr. Kent's office you came in few days ago. I wanted to know if you could come in order to discuss the results of your blood test and what you plan to do in terms of continuing the pregnancy."

Nyla forgot about taking a blood test. It came back so quickly. "Is everything o.k.?" She asked the nurse.

"You should come in as soon as you can, so we can figure out the next step in keeping you healthy." Not really answering the question, she was asked.

"Well I'm keeping the baby, and I thought the vitamins and iron pills were going to help me."

"Yes, but you will need more medicine to help with the disease through your pregnancy."

Nyla was confused as to what the nurse was talking about, "Disease, What disease?"

"Didn't you get the certified letter, we sent to you?"

Nyla remembered signing for the letter just a day ago, but she was in such a rush trying to handle some things that she just threw it in the drawer and left. "No, I mean I got it, but I haven't opened it yet. What's going on?"

"I can't tell you over the phone you just have to read the letter, and it will answer your questions."

"Look just tell me what's going on." She raised her voice yelling at the nurse "I'm sorry, can you please tell me what this is about, I promise I will not tell that you told me over the phone, I swear." She said as she calmed herself down.

"Ms. Carrolton, I'm sorry but you have full-blown AIDS."

"What!" Nyla screamed, "No, there's a mistake. You have to take the test again." Crying and acting hysterical. As classy as she appeared and as beautiful as she was, she had been around with more than a few one-night stands.

"The test is accurate. We run the AIDS test twice to be sure before we tell our patients such news."

Nyla grabbed the letter out of the drawer of the wooden coffee table and read it. It had confirmed everything the nurse had just told her. She balled the letter up and threw it down on the table.

"Hello, Ms. Carrolton are you still there?"

Tears began to run down her face and there was a moment of silence. She couldn't believe what she was hearing. "Thank you so much." She whispered as the phone slipped out of her hand and fell to the floor, wiping the tears from her eyes. As the phone fell the sound of her cell phone rang, it was Tre. She looked over at the phone trying to pull herself together as she wiped her tears from her face and cleared her throat, she answered the phone. "Hello"

"Hey, what's up?" Tre answered on the other end of the receiver.

"Hey" she replied with a choked up voice and a lump in her throat

"So what are you doing right now, I was thinking I could come through for a little something, something. Is that cool?"

"Umm, yeah, yeah come on through, I'll be waiting." She said as if she was a little unsure.

"Aiight, I'm on my way." Tre said

She hung the phone up and sat there thinking and contemplating on what to tell Tre. *Should I tell him about the baby? What about the AIDS? Damn, what am I going to do?*

Tre arrived at her apartment and knocked on the door. Nyla took a minute before she answered. "Damn, what's up" Tre said stopping in front of her.

"I need to talk to you about something."

"Talk to me about what? What's up? Why you stalling?"

Nyla swallowed hard and said to him, "I'm pregnant with your baby." She blurted out not even thinking about what she had just said.

Tre's eyes became squinty as the look of anger came upon his face. "What! What are you talking 'bout? I don't have time for this shit, these bull shit ass games you trying to play. I'm out." Tre started to walk off.

"It is not any game; I went to the doctor and found out a few days ago. I wasn't going to tell you, but I thought you needed to know."

"A few days ago you found out, and you telling me this shit now; bitch are you crazy? What, are you trying to do keep it?"

"Yeah, I am keeping it whether you like it or not." She told him with such aggression in her voice.

Tre became angrier, and he turned around grabbing his head not knowing what to do. *What is this bitch trying to do to me? Hell naw, I am not about to let this shit go down like that.* He turned around grabbing Nyla by the throat and pushing her into the apartment closing the door behind him. He turned and locked the door.

"What the fuck are you doing?" She started to yell at him.

Tre grabbed her by the throat again and squeezed as tight as he could, taking all of his anger out on her and slamming her into the wall while she was kicking and screaming. He put his hand over her mouth as she was yelling. "You just a fucking whore; trying to play me for a damn fool." The more he looked at her, the tighter he squeezed her neck.

Nyla's body had started to grow weak as she mumbled, "let me go, please."

"Oh now you don't like a nigga treating your ass like this, but you didn't mind when you let all of them niggas run-up in you like some animals and shit. You see; I know this 'cause you let me fuck the first day we met, within a few minutes. Now I supposed to believe this baby is mine." Her body became limp, and she was no longer kicking and screaming or even putting up any kind of fight.

"You gonna get an abortion, and then you better keep your mouth shut or next time you won't be so lucky." Tre took his hand from Nyla's throat. Her body dropped down to the floor. "Get your ass up" She didn't respond "Get up bitch" He started kicking her, but she did not move. Tre's bent down and felt her neck for a pulse. You could see the red bruise from where he had choked her. *Oh shit she's dead; I killed her.*

Tre stood up and looked around the room not knowing what he should do. He saw the phone lying on the floor by the couch. *Damn what if somebody is on the phone, and they heard me.* He walked over and picked up the phone but there was a dial tone. He placed it on the receiver and walked back to Nyla by the front door. He picked her up and placed her on the couch. Walking over to the window, he closed the blinds to make sure no one would see him. As he walked toward the door holding his head, he thought to himself. *Damn, I have to get rid of the body, but how? Where am I going to put it? I can't just leave it here. I have to get rid of the evidence.* His thoughts started to all come together at once.

As he looked around the room in a panic, he saw a certified letter envelope lying on the floor, and the letter lay out on the table. He picked it up and began reading the letter.

We regret to inform you that the test we performed on you, The AIDS test, was confirmed as positive. Please come by the office and/or contact us for more information about the results of your test.

"What the fuck!" Tre started to rub his head "Naw, hell naw this shit isn't for real." He turned towards the couch where he had laid Nyla's body and began shaking her. "Wake the fuck up bitch. This is what you do; get with niggas to give them your disease? Huh, you slut you hear me?" Grabbing her by her shirt and shaking her some more as if she is going to wake up and respond back to him. *O.k. think man what are you going to do with the body? Pull yourself together nigga.*

Looking at his watch, he sees that it is only six thirty. He grabbed the paper and put it in his back pocket along with the envelope to it then walked over to the kitchen table where the keys to Nyla's Jaguar sat. He placed them into his pocket and walked out of the front door closing it behind him, locking the door. *Good there's nobody out here.* Then he heard the sound of someone's whisper. "Tre" He looked around and up at the stairs to the sound of the voice but not seeing anyone. *My mind must be playing tricks on me.* He thought getting into his car and heading home. As he drove home, he continued thinking and contemplating about where he would dump the body. His mind was in a scramble, and he was beginning to feel overwhelmed with confusion. At this point, all he could think about is what the rest of his life would be like with AIDS.

Lovely came from around the corner where she had whispered into the wind Tre's name. She walked into Nyla's apartment and seen her lying on the couch coughing, struggling to catch her breath as she awakened from the state of passing out.

"What the hell happened here?" She said so nonchalantly as she stepped inside and closed the door behind her slowly walking over towards the couch.

"Lovely you have got to help me, he tried to kill me." Nyla could barely talk from the way Tre had choked her half to death.

"There, there, you know I'm going to take care of him for you just lay back and try to focus on catching your breath." Lovely stroked her hair. "Don't worry I'll get him. He will pay just like his brother. Now Nyla did you manage to find out anything about the money?"

"No I didn't get the chance to. I mean...." She began to cough some more. "Lovely I have to tell you something."

Lovely looked into Nyla's eyes with tears in them. "Yeah"

"I haven't been straight with you about everything. When I came up here I ran into Khalik a few times, and we got together. I was going to tell you but then your uncle had been killed, and I did not want you to have to have more things to worry about. Now that you know he had something to do with it I thought you should know." Nyla began to cough even harder.

"Shh," The look of rage came over Lovely's face. Her best friend, the only friend she had trusted to help her with one simple thing, and she could not even do that. Instead, she was more worried about being fucked, and she had been sleeping with Khalik all along. For all she knew Nyla was in on it too. Now all Lovely could think about is how much she had confided in her friend and how much she had known, which was a little much. She had to go. She had to get rid of her; it would be the only way.

Lovely stroked Nyla's hair once more and kissed her on the forehead. She then grabbed a pillow from the other end of the couch and placed it upon her face, smothering her. Nyla began to try to scream but the pillow muffled her screams. She tried fighting back but she was too weak, barely able to breathe from being choked to the very point of passing out and now being smothered with a pillow. She could no longer fight. Just clinging on by a single breathe. She let out her last muffled sound, and her body became limp. This time lifeless, Lovely killed her.

Lovely raised up from hovered over Nyla's lifeless body and began to look around the room. "Were the fuck can I put her?" She thought, but then remembered that Tre had taken Nyla's keys, so she knew that he would be back soon so she lifted her up from the couch and dragged her body down the hallway and into the room. She opened the doors and placed Nyla's body up against the wall inside of the closet.

"Now all I need to do is get to Tre, and he's all mines."

Tre waited until late that night as he got out of the bed, it was four o'clock in the morning. He put on some basketball shorts that were lying on the side of the bed by the hamper. He reached into the dark denim shorts that he was wearing and slowly pulled out the letter and Nyla's keys to her house and car. After putting on his shoes, Tre walked out of the house, down the stairs, and out of the building getting into his car.

It was Friday night, brothers were coming out shooting dice on the corner, music blasting, and the neighborhood bootleg house was packed with drunks trying to get a few shots of liquor. *Thirteen-year old girls out whoring with these old ass niggas, damn I cannot wait to get out of here.* He thought. Tre drove off passing all the bullshit that he could not seem to escape from living in the projects, from the grimy brothers, to the slumming. Tre pulled out of the Cabrini Green Projects and headed towards the highway and drove back to Nyla's, looking around to make sure no one was around. Tre unlocked the door to Nyla's place and went inside.

"What?" He said aloud to himself. "Where the fuck did she go?" Tre had left Nyla's body lying on the couch where he thought she was dead, but she was no longer there. He was confused and agitated; slowly, he seemed to be losing his mind all in one day. Tre walked around and looked in each room hoping that she had somehow woken up and crawled towards the back of the house, but she was nowhere in sight. As he stood there in Nyla's bedroom, he noticed an envelope on the bed with his name on it.

Tre, He read to his self. "Who knows I was here?" He opened the envelope and read it. *Meet me at the Drake Hotel, suite 1208.* Tre could not begin to know whom the letter was from or what they might have been trying to do, but he had to find out. Things were getting a little too bizarre.

Tre pulled up to Walton Street entering the Drake Hotel entranceway. He stepped out of the car while the valet parked it. As he entered the hotel "Damn" Tre was awe' struck he could not remember seeing something so big and beautiful. This is the type of place he wanted to be graced upon. The entrance was inviting and elegant with wainscoting in the hallways. Tre wanted this life. Tre walked over to the front desk.

"Is there something I can help you with sir?" The front-desk clerk asked Tre.

Uh, yeah could you tell me who's in the suit...?"

"Well hello there handsome."

"Lovely" Tre said as he turned around and looked in amazement. "We met before at the bank."

"Mr. Treshon I see you found me already huh," Looking at Tre very seductively with a smile.

Tre began to smile. "Wow this is something else. Funny that we are meeting like this." Becoming caught up in Lovely, he had completely been side tracked from the very reason why he was there at the hotel in the first place, not knowing that she was the one who left the note.

"Yeah well, let's just say that we happen to pass each other in the Palm Court, and I invited you up to my room, and of course, you had nothing to do, so you accepted." She told Tre sarcastically with a smile.

"Well, that seems nice but I supposed to be meeting someone in suite 1208."

"There's got to be some mistake because I'm in suite 1208, and I have been for a few weeks now."

Tre was confused, and he could feel his thought's racing. *That bitch, Nyla, she played me. Yeah just wait bitch, I am going to get your ass for real this time.* He thought, believing that Nyla had faked being dead when he choked her and is now playing games with him.

"On second thought, I think I will come and relax with you for a minute." They went up to the suit as Tre continued to admire the hotel.

"Here, how about a shot of Courvoisier." She poured them both a shot; making Tre's a double.

"Are you alright Tre?" She asked, looking into his dazed and confused eyes. Let me pour you a glass so you could relax a little." Lovely asked. Tre was starting to feel the effect of the alcohol, but he did not care. It has been a long time since he had been with a real woman. He gave the empty glass to lovely and continued to sit there admiring her as she walked over to the table in the room.

Grabbing the tall glass with a dark-red tint at the bottom of it lovely started pouring a glass of wine for Tre. She looked back to make sure he was not watching her. "Why don't you get a little more comfortable and take your shoes off."

"Yeah, alright I can do that." Tre said nervously.

Lovely waited until Tre turned around with his back to her then reached into the glass vase that was sitting on the table. She pulled out a small plastic sack with pills in it. *Ecstasy,* She thought. *It's about time I had myself a little fun.* She pulled out a blue pill with a Louis Vutton sign on the front of it and dropped it into the glass along with a little LSD. After watching it dissolve a bit she took the glass of wine back to Tre.

"Here you go. Here's a little pick up for you, make you feel even better." She said as she handed Tre the glass. *Yeah, I got you,* Lovely thought to herself as she suggested, "So Tre, why don't we get more acquainted." She implied with a seductive look on her face as she whispered into his ear. She lifted up Tre's hand and placed it on her breast.

"Why don't you go ahead and finish that," Knowing that she had put something into his drink. *This should start things off. The sooner I get close to him the faster I can get what is owed to me.*

Lovely looked around noticing that Tre's wallet was on the floor hanging out of his pant pocket. She opened it up to look inside. There was a picture inside of Tre with his brother. She thought, as she looked further through the wallet; nothing *an ID, driver's license, and bankcard.* As she looked into the other pocket of the wallet, she found some money. *Damn. Only forty dollars.* She knew that the amount of money she was looking for would not be hiding in his wallet, but she knew that she could find something from the bank or anything giving her some kind of clue as to where the money might be. Lovely noticed a letter that was for Nyla, it had explained everything, the reason why Tre had been so mad at her and tried to kill her. She gave him AIDS. She could not believe her eyes.

Tre began to wake up from the unconscious sleep he had been in. He squinted his eyes a few times to try to awaken. As he finally had gotten his focus, he looked across the room when he noticed Nyla lying next to him in the bed. He turned to get a closer look and noticed that her face had become very pale and turning a blue purplish color. He shook her with the only hand that he had free from being handcuffed to the bedpost, but her skin was cold...

"Fuck!" Tre yelled out.

"Oh, now Tre what's the matter? Lovely asked as she appeared from the bathroom.

"What the fuck is going on?"

"Well you see this is your little mess that I had to clean up. It's a shame too cause I thought she was my friend. I told her everything, and she played me for a fool just like your brother."

"My brother, what does Khalik have to do with this?" Tre asked with confusion.

"Your trifling brother slept with my best friend behind my back. Your brother killed my uncle and stole all of my money, and I want it back."

"What! There must be some mistake. Khalik did not kill anybody. Tre insisted.

"Where is my money?" Lovely asked

"Look, I don't know what you're talking 'bout, but you better get me out these handcuffs before things get real ugly in a minute."

"Really, and what are you gonna do? You see; you've already killed Nyla by strangulation, and now you're gonna turn the gun on yourself."

"You are a crazy bitch; let me out of these cuffs." Tre began to get angrier, spitting at her as he tugged to get free.

"There, there" Lovely walked towards him and pistol-whipped him across the head. She grabbed the cuff that hung from his wrist and unlocked it with the key, placing it in her pocket. Lovely pulled out her gun and aimed directly at the side of his head, towards the temple. She wanted to make it look as if he had killed himself after strangling Nyla.

"Say goodnight." Lovely gripped the gun with her black leather gloves and pulled the trigger and the splatter of blood scattered throughout the bed. The hole in his head seeped blood like a faucet of running water; covering the white sheets.

Now all I have to do is make it look more like a suicide. She thought. She placed the gun into Tre's hand and let it slowly drop to the ground, making it look as if he shot himself in the temple. Then Lovely took off the leather gloves and placed them into her purse, along with the cuffs that were in her pocket. She picked up any signs of her being there, went into the bathroom, and wiped the blood splatter from her face.

Lovely looked around to see if she had missed anything. She took the certified letter that was meant for Nyla and placed it into Tre's other hand as if he had been looking at it before he shot himself. Then she added a little more drink into his glass that sat on the nightstand next to the bed. She took a small syringe out of her purse and squeezed some of the liquor into it, releasing it into his throat.

Now I am done, let me get the hell out of here. She thought as she grabbed her purse and headed out of the front door. She had committed what would be the icing on the cake.

Cops surround the Drake Hotel and taped off the room to gather evidence in the homicide. Guest gathered towards the end of the long hallway trying to get a glimpse of what had happened. As police search and searched, the room had been cleaned of any evidence and not even a sign of fingerprints would be uncovered.

"Where's the lady who called into the front desk saying she may know something?" The lead detective on the case asked another officer.

"She's right over there talking to officer Barns," He said pointing over to the frantic woman.

The lead detective walked over towards the woman and interrupted the officer. "Excuse me ma'am, officer Barns I can take it from here."

"Yes sir." He responded and walked away.

"My name is Detective Larson, and I was wondering if you can tell me what you remembered about the incident."

"Well, I was sitting in the room watching my favorite show while my husband left out for a business meeting with some clients, and as I was sitting there I could hear these sort of muffled sounds of yelling coming from the wall, but I couldn't make out what they were saying. Then suddenly I heard a very loud bang. It sounded like a gun going off so I called the front desk and asked them if someone c come up and check things out to make sure, no one was hurt.

"Was there anything else that you could remember?" Larson asked.

"No sir, that was all." She replied. "My husband and I are only down here on business, and we always stay at this hotel. I'm really afraid that whoever did this may come back."

"Well, I understand how you must be feeling but this is in our hands now, and you have nothing to be afraid of. However, if there is anything else that you can remember, then, please feel free to give me a call day or night. Here's my card" He handed the woman his business card and walked away.

Larson stepped back into the room and stood over the body as the officer's and coroners collected evidence. While standing there he immediately began to feel as if it could just be a simple quarrel between two lovers who had gotten out of hand and the guy shot his girlfriend and then turned it on his self. The only witness was a neighbor in the other hotel room and judging from what she had heard and the way the bodies were it was lovers' quarrel gone too far.

"Detective here is the note we found in his hands. We are assuming this was the reason for the shooting." The officer said as he handed the plastic bag with the letter in it to him.

Larson grabbed the plastic bag with the letter in it and read to his self. He could see that the information contained in the letter was evidence pertaining to that of the woman lying in the bed next to the male victim. He had concluded that this was nothing more than what he had initially thought it to be, lovers' quarrel.

Detective Barns identifies the male victim as Treshon Givens and decides to notify the family. He picks up the phone and begins to dial from the list of numbers listed in Tre's phone. He reaches Khalik's number.

"Hey man where have you been, I have been calling you." Khalik immediately began to ask after picking up the phone when he noticed it was Tre's number that was calling him.

"Uh, hello this is Detective Barns I am looking for a Khalik."

"Yeah this is me. Who is this and what are you doing with my brother's phone, where he at?" Khalik questioned.

"If I can get you to come down to the precinct today I can explain everything to you, then." He said. "It is very important so it's imperative that I speak with you as soon as possible." Barns insisted.

Khalik became frantic. "The Police? Come down there for what? Where is my brother? What's going on?"

"This is not something that I would like to discuss over the phone." Barns told Khalik.

"Man look, what is going on?"

Barns took a long sigh. As much as he loved his job there were also parts that he hated and this was one of them. "I am sorry to have to tell you this, but your brother was found late last night at the Drake Hotel where he was pronounced dead at the scene from a gunshot womb to his right temple."

"What! Is this some kind of motherfucking joke or something? Put Tre on the phone for I have to bust your ass."

"I'm afraid this is no joke. We found your number in his phone. I am very sorry for your loss."

"Damn!" Khalik let out a horrific scream. Almost like a cry for help from pain and suffering endured. "Why? Why is this happening to me?"

"There was a young woman lying in the bed next to him, and she was also dead. Your brother had a letter in his hand, and we believe that the content of that letter is what caused him to kill her then caused a self-inflicted gunshot to the head." Barns explained.

Khalik was speechless and heartbroken from the news he has just received of his brother's death. What could he have done? Why hadn't he been there to protect him instead of being in the streets?

Officer Barns noticed how the silence grew longer. He finally said to Khalik, "Look I hate to have to do this…tell you over the phone I mean. However, you are going to have to come down to the precinct and identify the body. We have to be sure that he is who he is."

Khalik said nothing he only let out a big sigh. Then he said, "I don't think I could. I cannot see him like that. In a body bag or some sheet thrown over him like he's a piece of garbage about to be thrown away or something."

"I'm sorry but since you are the sole living relative then it has to be you. It's the only way." Barns shuffled through the papers that sat on his desk as he could hear the sounds of Khalik whimpering through the phone over the loss of his brother. He pulled out his schedule book from under the stack of papers and grabbed a pen from the jar that sat on his desk. "Okay, I would like for you to come down and identify the body this afternoon. What time could you be here?"

Khalik was silent and did not answer, but his breathing was loud enough to gather that he was still on the other end of the line.

"Hello, are you there? Mr. Givens? I know this is hard but the sooner we get this done the quicker you can begin to mourn and accept what has happened. Please if you can, I would like to see you this afternoon. It doesn't matter what time I will be here all night."

Khalik hung up the phone with the officer without even saying a word. As the hours continued to pass, he knew that eventually he would have to identify his brother's body, and it would be one of the hardest things that he would ever have to do in his entire life.

Khalik arrives at the morgue where he awaits for Barns so that he could identify his brother's body. As he sits and waits, his phone rings. "Hello" He answered.

"Hey man it's me, how you holding up?" Hassan asked.

"Shit, best as I can be. I still cannot believe this shit is happening right now. I mean. Why would Tre want to kill his self?"

"Yeah man none of this mess adds up. It seems so unreal. You know you and Tre are like my blood, my family, and if you need me to do anything just say the words. I got you."

"Thanks man. If I can count on anybody, it is you. I am down here at the morgue, and I am not so sure I can handle seeing him like that, all cold, and stuff, lying on a table with a sheet covering him. Fuck!" he shouted out.

"Say no more I'll be there in a minute."

"Naw, its cool thanks, but I got to do this myself. It's the only way I'm gonna be able to deal with this." He explained.

"Aiight, well get at me later man, and we'll kick it or something maybe go have a few drinks and share a few old stories." Hassan added.

"Yeah, I'll like that. Any ways, I've got to go so I'll get up with you later."

"Aiight"

Khalik hung up with Hassan and stared at the double doors as officer Barns walked through.

"Mr. Givens, I know it was hard but thank you for coming." Barns reached out his hand to shake Khalik's. They walked toward the back and walked through to the darkened room were Tre's body lay on a table.

"Hi, I'm Dr. David O'Neil, the chief medical examiner here." He clasped hands with officer Barns and Khalik. "I'm so sorry for your loss."

"Yeah whatever, let's just get this, over with so I can go. You think I want to sit here and stare at my brother like this." Khalik began to get hostile with the examiner.

"No of course not, my apologies," He walked over towards the table were Tre's body lay. Dr. O'Neil pulled the sheet back. "I'll leave you two for a second."

"Thanks Dr. O'Neil" officer Barns replied.

Khalik stood there still and frozen from what his eyes witnessed. Tre's body appeared pale and started to look like a corpse from the night of the living dead, only without all the gruesome peelings, cuts, and slashes. He had been covered with a whit sheet and had a tag that displayed his name on his big toe. Khalik reached out and touched his face. He gasped and then quickly moved his hand back. Tre's face was cold as ice. He looked up at officer Barns.

Barns could tell from the look on his face that he had just identified his brother. Before he could say a word, Khalik had already spoken.

"That's him." Khalik said, and he walked out of the room.

Officer Barns looked over at Dr. O'Neil and grabbed the paper from the clipboard that sat next to the table. He signed off on all the papers.

"Was there anything else I could do for you officer?" Dr. O'Neil asked.

"Yeah you know what get me a report of everything you have after you examine the body and have it sent to my office so that I can get a closer look at things." Barns replied. "Sure but I thought you guys were just ruling this as a suicide."

"Yeah we are but I just want to make sure everything is taken care of, and I'm gonna talk to my superior to rule out any possible further investigation."

Khalik walked out of the building and stood there against the brick. His chest had tightened, and his eyes became watery. He could feel his emotions, and anger builds up. Khalik had tears flowing from his face. He could not believe that his brother would take his own life. He felt as if he had no one left now except for Hassan. With his blood gone, he felt like he had failed. He failed his deceased mother and now his brother. Khalik felt that a big chunk had been taken from his heart and no matter what he would do, that chuck could never be replaced or restored. His world would come crumbling down, and this was only the beginning.

Chapter Eleven
Caught up

As the time went by Khalik, and Hassan managed to come up a little more. Working for Chavez put them on a new level of control and made them even more respected in Chicago. Hassan would take his monthly trips down to an abandoned warehouse where the cocaine and heroin were transported from Mexico to Chicago where they would re-up and exchange the money that they owed to Chavez. The drugs are distributed and the local street gangsters and others who work for Khalik and Hassan is who would push the dope out on the street. They also handle the work, but only to major clientele.

Hassan picked up the phone to call Khalik, "Yo Khalik, look, I'm gonna go take a little trip to Mexico tonight, and I'll be there for a few days."

"Damn man, we just got this shit and you're trying to go back to Mexico. That is the fourth time in the last month, almost every weekend your ass is going down there. Look, all I need you to do is wait until we get Chavez's money squared away, and then you can take a trip to Africa if you need to." Khalik told Hassan.

"Khalik man you don't need me to be here with you to run this for two days man, come on."

"I know I don't need you, but we got business to take care of first then you can take a trip if you want to. Why are you going up there any ways? You're going to see that bitch again aren't you?"

"I'm only going to be gone for two days."

"So what's up with you man, what's going on?" Khalik asked.

"I'll be back. I'm only gonna be gone for a few days and like I said you'll be good man, you handle this better than me anyway."

"That's not the point, man we supposed to do this together. We cannot do that if you are going to see some female every weekend. You are losing your focus on what we did all of this shit for anyway, Jimmy, those country ass niggas in Bama. We're trying to be two of the riches, most feared young niggas around the Chi, and you fucking off on some broad."

"Shit, we still gonna do that, I'm just taking some days off, not a few years." They both started to laugh at the paranoia that appeared from Khalik's voice.

"Aiight man I'll see you, but when you get back you make sure you got your head in the game." Khalik expressed.

"Aiight man, I'll hit you up when I get there."

"Aiight, later," Khalik said as they both hung up the phone.

"You want to be a whore and make your family ashamed, huh?" Chavez said slapping Jazell across the face so hard she dropped to the floor. "You go out and sleep with my runners. What, are they passing you around like a fucking piece of money?" The veins in his face began to protrude through his skin from the anger and rage he felt building up inside.

"No daddy, you don't understand. It's not what you think I love him." Jazell cried explaining to her father rising up from the floor.

You love him. You love him. This is why you've been lying to me and your mother so you can run back and forth to meet with him, to be his whore." Chavez slapped her once again, and again; she fell to the floor. "You are never to see him again, and I will make sure of it. Get her out of my site, Chavez told Juan. He knew that no matter what at the turn of his back, she would be gone. Out to be with him by any means necessary, sworn by the love that they formed. Even so, Chavez would not let this be, no matter what. His obligation was for his family, and his daughter was to be protected at all cost. He knew that the one way to do this was to kill Hassan. This would be the only way that he could keep them apart.

Juan helped her up off the floor and walked her back to her room, "You have to stay here because if you don't your father will kill him, do you understand?"

Juan had seen the look in her eyes, and he knew as well as her father that she would do exactly what she was forbade to do. She was a spitting image of him and to do other than what she wanted to would be unheard of.

Jazell looked up at Jose with tears rolling down her bruised cheeks, "I understand." She turned away, and Juan left out of the room.

Hassan gets a call from Jazell, "Hey. I was about to call you. I just got here and I'm headed to the room now."

"I will not be at our usual suite so meet me in room 408. I'll be waiting." Jazell said.

"Is everything alright, what's up?"

"Nothing, just meet me there, and I'll explain everything to you then."

"Aiight," As they hung the phone up, Hassan met Jazell in room 408 at their usual hotel. "Damn, baby what's up? You sounded like something was wrong with you on the phone."

"My father found out about us seeing each other."

"What! Oh fuck, what in the hell am I going to do?" Hassan began to panic. He knew that if he did not kill Chavez, then. He would kill him for messing with his daughter. "How the hell did he find out man. I thought you were being careful 'bout where you were going?"

"I was but my father is a well-known man, you know this. He could have easily been having someone keep an eye out for me or even keep an eye on you and Khalik. I am not sure, but we have to go somewhere before he finds you. If he finds you, he will kill you." Jazell was crying and shaking from a panic.

Hassan grabbed her by the arms, "Look we're not going anywhere.

We are just going to stay here for a few days, and I am going to call Khalik and let him know what is going on and tell him we going to need some more money. As long as we are checked in under another name, and we stay in this room until I figure out what we're going to do then they're not gonna find us, okay?"

Hassan wrapped his arms around Jazell as she continued to cry, shaking from the fear of what would happen. She knew what her father was capable of, and she knew that he was one of the most feared men, but Hassan was in love for the first time and there was nothing he would not do for her; even if it meant to kill her father.

Hassan got on the phone and called Khalik, "Yeah, hello." He answered.

"Khalik man it's me. I got a problem man, and I need you to get your ass down here as soon as possible." Hassan said in a frenzy and panicking voice.

"What the hell's going on? What happened? Where you at man?" Khalik could tell that from the tone of his voice that it was something serious.

"Look, I just got down here in Mexico and met up with Zell. He knows man."

"He knows. Who knows what? What are you talking 'bout?" Khalik asked becoming confused as to what Hassan was talking about.

"Chavez man, he found out that I have been seeing his daughter. I have to do something before he gets to me; I have to get him. I need your help man. I'm gonna kill him before he kills me."

"Awe shit, I told you to leave that bitch alone. Look, stay where you at. I am going to try to get the first flight out man. Don't do anything stupid, just chill until I get there."

"Yeah, aiight. Just make sure you get here before they kill me not after I'm already dead." Hassan said with sarcasm but in all seriousness."

"Yeah, I'll be there as soon as I can just sit tight man." They hung the phone up, and Khalik could already see how bad things were about to become. Everything was about to start quickly falling apart, and he wondered how they would pull out of this.

No later than a minute, after Hassan hung up the phone someone started to bang on the room door.

Jazell became nervous, "Oh my god who could that be? What if that's them, they're gonna kill us." She became very frantic.

Hassan placed his hands around her mouth. "Shh, just be quiet. If we do not say anything, they will go away. It's probably somebody with the wrong room number." The banging continued for a few more seconds, but no one was saying anything, then it finally stopped. "See, they're gone." He took his hands from around her mouth and looked into her eyes. "It's alright. I'm here, and I'm not going to let nothing happen to you."

Jazell wanted to believe him with all of her heart, but still she feared the worst. As they stood there hugging one another the silence quickly turned into mayhem with four masked men kicking down the door; holding guns.

Hassan quickly tried to reach for his gun but one of the men charged at him slapping him across the face with the gun; knocking him out cold.

Khalik tried his best to get a flight out but could not seem to get one that night. He called Hassan's cell phone to let him know that he will get their just to keep tight. As the phone rang someone answered the phone, but it was not Hassan.

"Well, well, we have been waiting for your call Khalik."

"Chavez, that's you?"

"I see you and your friend can't seem to follow directions very well. Your loyalty to me is very unsatisfying, and something must be done to fix it."

"Where is he? What did you do with hi Khalik started to raise his voice.

"It seems your little friend has been sleeping with my precious

Jazell behind my back, and now I will have to teach them both a lesson, not to mention the way you have been trying to steal some of my money; keeping it for yourself. You see I know and see everything, and nothing gets by me without me knowing about it. Your friend must die and soon you will too."

"What, steal some of your money. What in the hell are you talking 'bout?"

"Please, don't take me for the fool that you are."

"You fat motherfucker, I'll kill you, all of you. If you lay one finger on him." As he yelled into the phone, he could hear the sound of laughter and then a dial tone. *How am I going to get to him all the way in Mexico before they kill him, FUCK!* Khalik could only imagine the amount of torture, they had put Hassan though, but the problem is, he wondered, would he be able to get to him before they got rid of him.

Khalik's mind was racing. There was no way that he could get to Mexico that quick. He had no idea what he was going to do. As he stood there thinking and thinking, pacing back and forth, *"I can call Jose."* He thought. *Come to think of it. Where has this motherfucker been anyway?* Khalik picked up the phone to call Jose.

"Yeah, hello." Jose answered

"Yeah, man this Khalik. Where have you been?"

"Oh, shit, you know I've been 'round handling some things."

"Look, Hassan is there in Mexico right now and Chavez has got him strung the fuck up man, talking 'bout he is going to kill him. I need you to talk to your uncle and find out what is going on down there. I need your help man, for real." Khalik explained

"Oh, now you want my help." Jose said sounding high as usual.

"Man what are you talking 'bout? This shit is serious."

"Yeah, aiight, where you at now?" Jose asked

"I'm at the spot. Let me get these bitches straight" Khalik said referring to the bricks of coke, he had laid out in the house. "I'll give you a call where we can meet in about 20 minutes."

"Yeah, aiight." Jose hung up the phone and sat back puffing on a joint. *Yeah motherfucker, let us see how you get out of this. Fucking betrayed me.* He thought.

Khalik promised Hassan that he would always have his back just as he did for him, he let him down, and he could never forgive his self for what happened to Hassan. All he could do is get justice, and that is exactly what he planned to do.

Khalik could still hear the sound of Hassan's voice over the phone. Three years later and it angered him all over again. The last time he had spoken to his best friend who he had been through everything with and then suddenly he was gone, just like that. Khalik felt like it was all his faults, he never made it there.

In the basement of Chavez million-dollar home, made especially for anyone who got out of line, Hassan sat in the chair passed out; awakening from the big splash of water hitting his body, in pain with blood dripping from his forehead. Barely able to see he opened his eyes. He had been tied to the chair with rope and gagged with tape strapped over his mouth.

"Well, well, I see you finally want to wake up and join the party." Chavez said

Hassan looked; round the room and began to become terrified, squirming, and screaming behind the masked tape that covered his mouth, from the sight of the guns, knives, and gasoline tank. As he stared at all of that, he noticed that Jazell was nowhere to be found.

"Are you looking for Jazell? Well, she will not be joining us. However, don't worry I will be sure to give her a little remembrance of you when we're done." Chavez began to circle around Hassan "You see; this isn't only about you sleeping with my daughter. No, it is much more than that. You see; I know that you have been stealing money from me."

Hassan shook his head at what he knew was wrong. He had no idea that Jazell was the one and nor did Chavez.

"Oh, yes, you know perfectly well what I am talking about. It is just too bad that you thought I was stupid enough not to find out. You know; on second thought, I think maybe my little Jazell should join us for this considering it will be a lesson learned to the both of you. Juan, would you get her in here."

Jazell was in the other room with tape tied over her mouth. Juan brought her out and stood her in front of Hassan. He ripped the tape from across her mouth.

"You see what you have done. You remember him this way because this is what's gonna happen to anyone who crosses me." He yelled to Jazell.

She closed her eyes from the sight of Hassan beaten and bruised.

"Look at him!" He yelled out to her.

She opened her eyes with tears rolling down her cheeks. "No, please don't make me watch this. Please papa don't do this."

Chavez walked around her and grabbed the gasoline tank from the floor. He handed it to Juan. "Would you please do the honors?" He said

Juan splashed the gasoline all over Hassan.

"Now, let me take a try at this. Why don't you sit Jose, take a load off." Chavez told Juan.

He sat down in the chair, unsuspecting of anything that was about to happen. Chavez snapped his fingers. The two guards who were in the room rushed to Juan sitting in the chair. One of them held his hands behind his back while the other tied the rope around him. "Hey, what are you doing?"

"You didn't think I was going to let you get away with this too now did you? After all someone had to pay for bringing these low lives into my house and someone has to be responsible for this. Why not you? I mean you were the one who brought them here."

"No, you don't understand..." Juan began to talk but was

quickly gagged.

"I can't very well hold your nephew responsible, so I am going to hold you responsible." Chavez took the gasoline tank and poured what was left of the gas all over him. "Buenos notches boys." Chavez began to walk away as each of the guards lit a fire to both Hassan and Juan. The screams were unbearable. "Take her up to her room."

They grabbed Jazell and took her to her room. Chavez walked away leaving them to burn alive in the basement, closing the door behind him. He started to walk up the stairs when his wife met him at the top.

"Is everything o.k.?" She questioned

"Everything is fine. It is none of your concern, go on back to bed I'll be up shortly." He gave her a stern voice and a cold look. All the years of their marriage she knew what had happened and would turn away and never to ask questions about what was happening.

Behind the closed doors where Hassan and Juan were left to burn, the fire began to settle down, and the screams begin to fade. There they both lay in the basement tied, gagged, and burned.

Thinking of Hassan's death made Khalik think of his brother Tre and how he failed him. He had no one left, and he knew he had to do something, but no matter what it was not going to bring his family back, nor was it going to take away the pain.

As soon as he hung the phone up with Khalik, Jose picked up the phone again and called Smith on his cell.

"Hello" Smith answered

"Yeah, you got your boy this time all you have to do is go and get him." Jose confirmed

"Where?" He is at his place right now with enough coke to put his ass away for a long time.

Jose gave the address to Smith and they both hung up the phone.

As he got off the phone, Jose decided that he would go and get in on the action by watching closely from across the street. *How sweet it would be to see that motherfucker burn.* He thought. *Na, I'd better not. Any ways he deserves just what he gets, him, and Hassan.*

Khalik continued to load up the bricks of cocaine he had been laying out when he paused. He could hear the sound of police sirens in the air. *What in the hell,* He thought. Khalik looked out the window to see two police cars posted up and the officers standing outside, walking towards the door. J then one of them started to bang on the door.

"Police open up" the officer said

Khalik did not know what to do. The only person who knew he had this at his house was Hassan, and he knew it was not him. He had been held in Mexico, and he was the reason Khalik was trying to rush to go. The only person who could have had something to do with it was Jose. *That snake ass motherfucker.* Khalik continued to look 'round the room and think of what his next move would be, but he could not see anything.

"Alright, were coming in" The officers burst through the door.

Khalik stood there not knowing what he would do. The sound of the officers screaming at him with guns pointing towards him and sirens wailing were drowned out by his thoughts. Hassan was depending on him. Tre was his only family, and he was depending on him. He could not let them down.

"Put your hands in the air and get down on the ground." The officer yelled out.

Khalik looked over to see his gun lying on the table. He reached and grabbed it then began to shoot. One of the officers was hit in the arm while the other two ducked for cover. Khalik did not see the third officer as he crawled from behind the door and tackled him to the ground, knocking the gun out of his hand. It was Smith. He grabbed

Khalik's hands and placed them behind his back putting the handcuffs on extra tight.

"Hello ass hole" Smith spoke into his ear as he pulled him up from the ground. "You know where you're going? Huh, to the slammer that's where. You know they like pretty boys like yourself." Smith began to laugh. "Alright boys let's wrap it up." He said to the other officers who wanted to kick the life out of Khalik for almost taking theirs. Smith grabbed Khalik's arm tightly and headed towards the door, walking him to the car. "Well, well, what a stupid mistake you've made. Your friend Jose sure does know how to deliver doesn't he."

Khalik looked up at Smith and gave him the coldest look he had ever seen. "I'm going to get him right after I get you." He said

"Yeah, the only thing you're going to be getting is a trip to the commissary every week." Smith laughed at his own joke.

Khalik felt the anger build up inside of him. Jose sold him out, and his best friend could be half-dead by now. He knew he had to get his revenge, but the reality was that he would be in jail for a long time and there was nothing he could do.

Back at the precinct, Smith began to process the paperwork on Khalik.

"Detective Smith you have a call holding on line two," Yelled out one of the other cops in the precinct.

"Hello, this is Detective Smith" he said answering the call.

"Detective Smith this is Lovely, how are you?"

"Well, long time no hear from, I was beginning to think you forgot about our little deal." Smith replied.

"Meet me at the coffee shop in say, 10 minutes." Lovely told Smith as she hung the phone up.

As Detective Smith walked out of the precinct, Shanell sat in the car across the street waiting for him. She planned to follow him and then kill him. She followed Smith and watched as he went into the coffee shop and walked towards the very back where lovely was sitting. Her beauty mesmerized him once again. He sat down, "Well, well, the last time I heard from you was a brief two-minute phone call letting me know that things were going o.k. then nothing else for almost a month now."

"Look, I'm gonna get them, It just takes time, but I wanted to see you personally to let you know that I have got them right where we want them, and soon they will be yours, that is unless you're giving me the o.k. to dispose of them myself. As a matter of fact, I just brought Khalik in on drug charges, so he is in there for a long time."

"What good is he to me if he's in jail?" Lovely asked, "He has my uncle's money that he killed him for, and I can't get that with him in jail. Besides, if I don't get that money you don't get your cut." She said

"Yeah well he would need the key....." Smith stopped himself from what he was about to say.

"What did you say?" Lovely could not believe what she was hearing, but then nothing seemed to be unbelievable now. So she questioned him of his words.

"Well, I was just saying that he would need to keep his eye out in prison because anybody can get hurt." Smith covered up what he had really said.

Lovely was not stupid by far, and she knew right then that she was in this alone. No one could be trusted, especially not some prejudice law. However, she already figured that from the beginning. Lovely did not care what it took, and she would get rid of anyone who would get in her way.

Smith looked at Lovely and gazed into her eyes leaning towards her. "Just as long as the job gets done then it really doesn't matter which of us does it, as long as where happy with the results, right."

Lovely leaned back in towards Smith barely touching his lips with hers, "Right'" She whispered "What do you say about meeting me at the motel a block over from here in about 15 minutes, room 118." She stood up from the table and walked off hoping that he would take her up on her offer.

Smith turned around from the booth that they both sat in watching as Lovely walked away. He sat and thought for a second. *This is a fucking nigger, what am I doing? Damn, forget it, who is going to know any ways. I'll make this bitch fall in love with me, and after she does my dirty work then she'll be going down with the rest of them, I'll put all they're asses in there at the same time buried up under the jail. Fewer niggers out here on our street,* Smith rose up from the table and walked out of the coffee shop.

Shanell watched as the beautiful black woman walked out and Smith right behind her. *I wonder if he is following her.*

Smith got into his car and began following not too far behind Lovely. Shanell would be right behind the both of them. They pulled up to the hotel, and Smith stepped out of his car and slowly followed behind Lovely up the stairs to room 118. He knocked on the door. Shanell sat back in the car wondering who she was and what was going on. She knew that he was a prejudice law and getting anywhere near anybody of another race outside of work meant it was something in it for him.

Lovely opened it with a red-laced negligee on pulling him into the room pulling at his clothes in a hurry to get them all off him. Naked and standing there, Smith threw lovely onto the bed and turned her over on her stomach snatching the crotch of the negligee open. Smith positioned his self with his penis in his hand ready to insert it and holding her head down into the pillow on the bed as if he was going to rape her then he grabbed her by her waist and pulled her forcefully towards his penis.

"Wait, I almost forgot something." Lovely interrupted him as he was about to place his self-inside of her.

"What?" He questioned.

Lovely slowly turned over as she reached her hands under the pillow that her face laid smashed in and pulled out a gun. She rose up from the bed and placed the gun to Smiths head.

What's going on? Smith said nervous sure, that she would use the gun.

Lovely got closer to him, and she placed her gun to Smith's head touching his forehead.

"Turn around and get on your knees." She told him.

Smith turned around and got on his knees. "Look, your making a big mistake. Just let me talk to you and show you."

"Shut up!" Lovely told him in a rage as she looked at him straight in the eye with the gun pointing at his head, "Now tell me what happened to the key that my uncle left in the safe. You tried to take my shit too, and you thought that you would get away with it, didn't you?"

"Look, just put the gun down and we can talk. Remember we have a deal. You don't even know how those nigg...." He caught his self from the words that were about to come from his mouth. This was all Whitman's idea, for all we know he could be behind your uncle's murder. He's probably working with Khalik and Hassan, and now he's trying to kill you." Smith started talking trying to get into her head, thinking that she would be so naive as to believe him. "That's why I can get rid of him, so we could be together. No one would know once we got rid of everyone. I am a cop so you know I can take care of the evidence. There's nothing to worry about."

She knew of his untrustworthiness, so not for one minute would she believe anything that he was saying. Lovely took the gun from his forehead and placed it between his eyes. "Now, where is the key and who in the fuck has my money."

"O.k. look, I found a key in the safe in your uncle's house, so I went to the bank to see if there was anything that would help me to put those two ass holes in jail. That's when I looked in the safe and realized that it was 10,000,000 in it. I took the money and I was going to give it to you, but I guess I was just so excited to hear from you that

I completely forgot it. I haven't been able to stop thinking about you since I first laid eyes on you." Smith began to make things up trying to win her over.

"Where is the money, now?"

"If you let me put my clothes on, then I'll take you right to it."

"Do you think I'm stupid, huh, where is the money?" Lovely asked him once more.

"O.k. it's at my house in a suitcase in the closet. If you let me call my wife, I'll have her bring it to you."

"Fuck you, redneck motherfucker, this is for my uncle." Lovely fired a shot right between his eyes blowing a hole straight through his head as his lifeless body fell to the floor. She reached into her purse, pulled out the plaque from her uncle's house, and bashed his head in with it, leaving it on the ground lying next to his body.

Outside, Shanell could hear the sound of a loud blast, but she ignored it, still waiting for Smith and the unknown woman to appear.

"And this is for thinking I'm some stupid whore." She fired once again, hitting him in the chest, straight through the heart, "Heartless bastard," Standing over him with vengeance. Less than 20 minutes after they both walked in, lovely walked out of the motel, Shanell noticed that Smith was not behind her.

Chapter Twelve

Secrets

Jamel had made his escape from the prison grounds, and by now, they were well past just looking for him. A nationwide search had been, in effect, for what was considered a dangerous escapee from prison. Over the course of the next few days, hiding out would be hard but Jamel did not care. He managed to learn a few tricks while in prison and knew just how to get quick cash. Fortunately, for him, he had seized the wallet of the guard he robbed and managed to get some money to get him over for a while before doing away with all the guards' identification. He was on a mission in finding out who killed his brother and to learn what had happened.

Jamel sat on the edge of the bed and turned on the television to watch the ten o'clock news.

"Our top story today is the death of long time police veteran Detective Phil Smith, who was found, shot to death in the Best Western Motel with a single gunshot wound to the head and another to the chest. Police believe that this crime is related to drug lord Jimmy Johnson, who was also killed recently in his luxury home. Police say that Detective Smith's partner has been missing, and no one knows of his last-known whereabouts. They have not been able to contact Smith's wife since the discovery and are ruling this as a possible homicide. So far, police refuse to release any more information in this case until they have further investigated. They are, however, asking if anyone knows anything about the whereabouts of Detective Beau Whitman and Shanell Smith or the death of Detective Phil Smith to contact the Illinois Police Department." The news anchor stated.

Wife, Shanell Smith, I cannot believe she married that cracker motherfucker.

I have to find her. He thought.

Shanell continued to trail behind Lovely after she left the motel and already the news of Smith's death had spread by that night. She was shocked, the last time she had seen him was following in the motel with that woman whom she had no idea who she was. She knew that Smith was crooked and no good, but she never knew if she were able to see the day that somebody would finally get to him before he got to him or her.

Who is she? Shanell thought as she sat outside in the car still covered with Whitman's blood all over her clothes crept off in a dark area of the street watching as Lovely pulled in near the Drake hotel next to the Oak Street Beach.

Lovely got out of the car and walked over towards the water on the beach. *Now all I need to do is get rid of this.* She looked around and pulled the gun she killed Smith with earlier that day out of her purse and threw it into the water. She hurried back towards her car and drove off, not realizing the whole day that someone had been following her.

Jamel pulled up to see some of his friends at the store in one of the old neighborhoods of his.

"Hey, what's up nigga, your face been all over the news, and you're out here chilling with us. Gutsy motherfucker." The man said to Jamel.

"Shit, look, I had to get leave that damn place when I found out about Jimmy." Jamel said

"Yeah man, I still can't believe it."

"I'm still trying to find out who this bitch is that's asking 'bout my brother and why."

"As a matter of fact, a matter of fact she came 'round here last night after you left talking 'bout some money them niggas stole from

her and how she had a reward for anybody who bring them to her."
The other man said.

"Who?" Jamel asked

"Khalik and Hassan, they were two of Jimmy's best boys. Shit,
those little niggas could talk a trick out of a treat. You hear what I'm
saying." The old timer added.

"Yeah, she wrote down her number and gave it to us." He reached
into his pocket and pulled out his wallet searching for the number.
Here it is." The man gave the number to Jamel.

"Yo, isn't that her car right there?" The man said pointing in the
other direction.

"Yeah that's her."

"Are you sure?" Jamel asked

"Yeah" The man said.

"Aiight, I'm gonna get up with y'all later." As Jamel began to walk
off the man stopped him.

"Yo man, you might need this. There's no telling what that bitch up
to." He reached behind him, pulled the gun from his pants underneath
his shirt, and handed it to Jamel.

"Good look in'." Jamel hurried to get into the car that an old friend
of his who owed him a favor back then let him have. It was not anything fancy, but Jamel did not care as long as he had something to get
around in and to keep him out of sight with the cops. Jamel hurried to
catch up with the car, but could not seem to get past the car that was
in front of him.

Lovely turned the corner at the stoplight and so did Shanell. Jamel
turned also, following behind the two. *Damn this car needs to move out of
the way.* He thought.

Lovely finally noticed that the car behind her was tailing her, but
she did not see the car that Jamel was in. *Who is this following me? Maybe
I am just tripping.* Lovely ignored her feeling and drove to an old area
where her uncle used to take her growing up, overlooking the water.

She pulled over and got out of the car. She had not been there in years, but she still remembered how it made her feel each time she was there. It was their special place together. As she stood out looking into the water, Lovely noticed the sound of another car pulling up, but she saw no lights.

Shanell slowly pulled up far behind Lovely and parked towards the bushes with the headlights turned off. *Shit, where did she go?* Lovely vanished. *She was just standing there.* Shanell thought. She noticed car lights pulling up behind her. She ducked down into her seat.

It was Jamel; He parked the car and got out, wondering where the woman had gone. He walked past the car Shanell sat in looking into the dark tinted windows, but could see nothing then he began to walk off towards the water, looking for the woman.

Shanell noticed the man looking into the window before he walked off, hoping that it was too dark to see. She got out of her car slowly and shut the door when no sooner someone grabbed her from behind choking her with a gun to her head, walking towards the water where Jamel stood looking around.

"Who the fuck are you and why you're following me?" Lovely demanded

Shanell was scared she knew nothing about this woman or what she was capable of.

Jamel turned to see the woman behind him pointing a gun with another woman held hostage. *What the fuck.* He thought

"Who the hell are you and why are y'all following me?"

Jamel looked at her. He was confused. "What? Look I don't know who she is."

"Bullshit." Lovely said as she gripped her arm tighter around Shanell's neck and placed the gun on Jamel.

Jamel took the gun the man had given him and pointed it at Lovely. "Like I said I don't know who the fuck this bitch is, and I don't know who you are, but what I do want to know is why you're going 'round asking 'bout my brother." Jamel began to walk closer up on her while the both of them still had their guns on one another, but not close enough for Shanell to notice who he was.

"Your brother stole 10,000,000 dollars from me, and I want it back." Lovely said thinking that he was Hassan's brother because she knew that Khalik had only had one brother, and that was Tre.

"What? Bitch my brother had money he didn't have to steal nothing from nobody." Jamel began to walk even closer. "Now I suggest you quit fucking 'round and tell me who in the hell you are and what the fuck you know 'bout what happened to my brother.

Shanell's eyes became wide, but she could barely speak from the grip that was around her neck. She began to squirm when she finally got Lovely's arm from around her. "Jamel?"

Lovely let go. "Don't try shit bitch or I'll put a hole in your ass right along with him."

Shanell ignored lovely with her back still turned away from her. "What, where did you…"

Jamel looked. He could not believe his eyes. After all, of these years she was standing in front of him.

"I'm so sorry about what happened to Jimmy?" Shanell said

"Jimmy?" Lovely repeated

"Yeah, Jimmy Johnson"

"What? Who are you? Somebody better tell me what is going on and what my uncle has to do with this."

"Uncle," Jamel and Shanell said at the same time looking at Lovely

"Yeah, Jimmy Johnson was my uncle, and I've been looking for the two motherfuckers who killed him, Khalik and Hassan. That slimy Detective Smith told me who did it. Who killed my uncle and they are gonna pay."

"Wait a minute, if Jimmy was your uncle, then…." Shanell began before being interrupted by Jamel.

"This is some bullshit ass game you fucking playing and…" Jamel said

"Hold on just wait a minute. Smith killed him. He had those boys set him up." Shanell said, "Years ago Jimmy was making so much money that this crooked cop bribed him for a piece of what he was making every month or we all were gonna be sent to prison for a very long time. To keep him off our backs Jimmy agreed until the cop wanted more. He wanted me; he could not accept the fact that a white woman was working for some black street hustler, one night at Jimmy's house Smith came, and forced me to go with him. I respected and cared for Jimmy and his crew so much that I wasn't going to let anything happen, so I agreed to anything he wanted as long as he left them alone, and that was the night Smith set Jamel up and sent him to prison."

"So what does this have to do with me?" Lovely asked

"Well, you see; I was pregnant and Smith wouldn't let me keep the baby, so I begged for him to let me give it to someone who I knew would take care of it. Jimmy was the only person that I could trust to do that. So when I gave birth to my baby girl, I gave her to Jimmy. That was the last time that I saw Jimmy or my daughter then I heard that he had been killed. When I found out, I confronted Smith and found out about the money that he and his partner had stolen from Jimmy. I managed to find the money and took it. So, you see, the little girl was you. You're my daughter." Shanell continued to explain to Lovely.

"Wait a minute, what!" Jamel was in disbelief.

"You bitch, you lying bitch. You were in on this with Smith, and you had my uncle killed. You just made up this story to cover your ass."

"No I promise you...." Shanell was interrupted.

"You stole my money. Didn't you? Where is it, huh, where is it?" Lovely began to yell hysterically at Shanell while walking closer up on her.

"It, it's in the car but..." No sooner than the words flowing from her tongue, Lovely fired a shot once at Shanell, hitting her in the abdomen. Shanell fell to the ground.

"No" Jamel yelled out pointing his gun and aiming for Lovely

Shanell lye on the ground bleeding badly, near to death she screamed out to Jamel "No, Jamel stop. She's your daughter...." Nevertheless, before she could finish her words Jamel had struck lovely straight in the chest.

He could not believe his ears. Jamel rushed to Shanell, gently picking her head up from the ground and placing it in his lap. "Awe no Shanell, please tell me that isn't true, Shanell please." Jamel begins to cry.

Shanell started to gurgle blood, barely clinging on to life. "I'm so sorry." She mumbled to him. Her eyes began to roll back.

"Shanell, don't leave me, I can't lose you too." He cried out to her, but she was already gone. Jamel was hurt. The pain of his heart was too deep, almost unbearable. He placed his hand over her face and closed her eyes, then laid her back on the ground. As he rose up, he stopped and took a long look at his daughter, the daughter whom he never knew, and the daughter that he had just killed. He bent down and kissed her upon her forehead with a single tear running along his cheek. Then he rose from the ground and began to walk back towards the car.

As he walked to the car, Jamel remembered that Shanell said she had the money that was missing. He walked over to her car and opened up the door. There in the front seat upon the floor was a bag. He opened it up to take a look inside, and there it was. It was the money his daughter was looking for, Jimmy's money. He took the bag from the car and got into his. Jamel had no idea where he would go or what he would do, but he knew that he could not stay there, he was a wanted man. A wanted man with no one to share his life with, a life that he would soon start over.

Chapter Thirteen

Getting Out

Jose sat in his apartment watching Scarface on T.V. when someone knocked on his door. *Damn who is this,* He thought. Jose got up from the couch and walked towards the door. When he answered, he noticed a beautiful Hispanic woman at the door. Aye mama, He said.

"Hi, is Maria home?" She said

"Maria? There is no Maria that stays here but what can I do for you?" Jose asked, basking in her presence.

"Well, I was trying to stop by and say hello to a friend of mine from work, and I thought this was the address that she gave me. I am sorry to bother you."

"Oh, no bother at all. It is a pleasure to see such a beautiful woman in my presence for a change. Would you like to come in for a drink or something?" Jose said trying to turn on his charm.

The woman walked slowly up towards him and kissed him passionately on the lips.

Jose was stunned "Damn ma."

She stepped back and looked at Jose with a smile, then leaned in towards him and whispered into his ear "I don't want a drink, but I do want something else." She said before stepping back.

Jose opened the door wider to let her in. After closing the door, he turned back around "So what is it that you want?" He asked

"Come here and I'll show you." She started to undo the buttons of her dress, letting her breast peek through.

Jose walked closer towards her and buried his head on her chest. "Oh yeah, this must be a dream cause I'm in heaven." He said enjoying the view.

She reached behind her back and pulled a blade from the back of her bra. "You're not in heaven, but you are going to hell." She said. As he looked up at her, she plunged the blade into his throat. She pulled the blade out and pushed him onto the ground, standing over him, watching as the blood began to come out of his mouth, and he struggled for help, but could not speak. "You see; word on the streets is you telling on your boys. Those same boys who were always down with you, here is a little message. Keep your mouth shut."

Jose crawled into the kitchen and grabbed on the drawer, trying to get it open, but he fell onto the floor, gurgling on his own blood.

She walked over to the drawer and opened it. Sitting in there was a gun. "Oh, you were planning on using this on me huh." She closed the drawer shut and stabbed Jose once more in the throat, killing him this time. Then she pulled the blade out, cut his tongue out of his mouth, and threw it on the ground. "I guess you won't be using this to tell on anybody else." Jazell walked over to the kitchen and got a napkin. She wiped the blood from the blade then buttoned up her dress and walked out of the house.

"Givens, let's go." The guard came to the cell to get Khalik. "You know the routine."

Khalik rose up from his bunk, turned around, and placed his hands through the slot on the cell door. The guard handcuffed him.

"Alright, come on." The guard opened the cell door as Khalik walked out. He followed behind Khalik where another guard walked in front, leading the way.

"Sit here." The guard said as he sat Khalik on the bench. One of them knocked on the door. The door opened. It was the warden. "We have Khalik Givens here when you're ready for him."

"Alright bring him in." The warden said to the guards. They lifted Khalik up from the bench he sat on and walked him into the room where members of the parole board were sitting.

"Have a seat Mr. Givens." The woman told him pointing to the chairs in front of them. The guard unlocked the handcuffs and took them off of Khalik while still standing behind him to ensure that he wouldn't try to make any sudden moves. Khalik rubbed his wrist, relieved from the tight cuffs around them. He sat in the chair facing the members of the parole board; the very same people who would decide his fate and give him the chance to be free. "Recently Mr. Givens we sent you a letter letting you know that we would review your case, and it seemed to us that there may have been some discrepancies involved. In the event of your arrest, the on-duty officers who arrested you did not take all the proper procedures required by law when making an arrest."

"Uh, excuse me ma'am I don't mean to interrupt, and I'm sorry for that, but I don't understand what you mean." Khalik expressed

"Well, Mr. Givens, the officers who placed you under arrest somehow forgot to Mirandize you." Confusion grew upon Khalik's face. "In other words, they forgot to read you your rights. I do not know exactly how it was even missed seeing is how it is all written here in the paperwork. Apparently, one of the officers stated to the arresting officer that he forgot to read you, your rights, and he never got around to do it, I guess. Since that officer is no longer with us, then we cannot go further into investigation and the state of Illinois feels that you have served a good enough term. You broke the law and should be serving a longer term; nonetheless, we have to let you go."

"In the upcoming days of your granted release we are required to talk to you about the consequences of any violation of the terms of your parole. If you shall violate you will be immediately sentenced to the maximum sentence given to you by the judge. If you may encounter any situation, you shall take it up with the laws of this state and not yourself. This means that there will be no retaliations of any kind with those who are also on parole, no dealings of drugs, no alcohol use, no committing any thefts, burglaries, rapes, or murders, for that matter. Do we make ourselves clear?"

"Yes" Khalik answered

"And you do understand your rights, the laws, and rules and regulations with what you must abide by, correct?" She continued.

"Yes I do understand"

"Now, I would assume that we are all clear on things so is there anything that you needed to add before we let you go on Mr. Givens?"

Khalik looked at the warden as he finished his speech. "No. There isn't." He said politely, biting his tongue from wanting to say what he really felt. *It took you crackers three years from my life to let me up out this bitch.*

"Alright then, due to the overcrowding in the Illinois State Penitentiary your date will be moved up, and you're scheduled for release one week from today. Now I need you to sign these papers and hopefully this will be our last encounter." The warden confirmed.

Khalik signed the papers that the warden placed in front of him.

"If there isn't anything else, then you can take him back to his cell." She stated to the guards.

"Come on." The guards walked Khalik out of the room as they pulled him up from the seat and walked him down the halls of the prison building. He felt nothing, no joy, no happiness, nothing. He wanted to be completely free, and he was not happy until he got there.

A week had passed and as that time went by Khalik still felt nothing of joy, just anxious. "Givens, times up." The guard yelled. "You know the routine."

Khalik turned to keeper and gave him a nod. Keeper nodded back. Neither of them had to speak, the words were already there. Now he was happy. As pleased, as he was to be leaving he was actually going to miss keeper, and the feeling was mutual. They had shared a cell for most of his time in, and now he was finally getting out. Khalik turned around and placed his hands into the slot on the cell door as the guard placed the handcuffs on him, he could feel them tightening around his wrist. As he turned around to exit the cell, the doors opened up.

"Alright, boy we don't want to see your black ass back here." The overweight guard said, knowing almost every inmate in there he had been there so long.

Walking down the long hallway passing by all the inmates Khalik could not believe all that was happening. In just a short time, he would be walking through the doors to the outside world and there was no turning back. The guard walked him down to processing. Khalik sat there waiting in cuffs as the woman finished processing his release into the computer.

"Alright if I can get him to sign here, then you can get your things, and you're free to go." The country white woman said with an out-of-town accent.

The guard took the cuffs off Khalik's wrist. "Alright, don't try anything funny because you're not out of here yet, and I will be glad to lock your black ass back up."

Khalik removed his wrist grabbing and rubbing them. He picked up the pen and signed the papers.

"Alright, here are your things, if you sign one more form for me saying that we released your property, and then you're done." She said. "You'll want to make sure all of your stuff is in there."

Khalik signed the last paper and grabbed his things. There were two bags, one with his clothes and the other was an envelope with 100.00. He opened up the bags. *Damn, 100.00 dollars to my name.* The guard took Khalik to a room nearby to change into his belongings. As he finished he stepped out and the guard escorted him to the front entrance to the prison.

"Open up." The guard yelled out as one of the guards who worked the front entrance door opened up the doors for Khalik, "So long asshole." The guard told him.

As he walked out the doors to the prison, the light from the sun graced his dark skin, beaming through his chestnut brown eyes. Khalik was finally happy. He smiled, for three years, he had been imprisoned, and the day he had awaited was here. He was a free man from the Illinois State Prison but not from the caged fury that was buried deep in his heart.

As Khalik stood outside of the Illinois State Prison. A white 57' Chevy Bel Air with tinted windows pulled up alongside of him. He could not believe his eyes. *Am I dreaming?* He asked his self. Khalik continued looking, staring into the eyes of the man who would be his long-time friend Hassan.

Hassan rose from out of the car and walked towards Khalik, who was still stunned and frozen with disbelief. "Man I thought you would be happy to see me alive." Hassan said

"Wait a minute, I must be losing it. All that time in that shit hole must have clouded my thoughts and vision. How are you alive? What are you doing here? How come you never contacted me? I thought you were dead." Khalik stopped and took a deep breath then smiled and looked at Hassan, still with a surprised look upon his face. They clasped hands and hugged. This was more than just a good day this was the best day of his life in the last three years.

"It's me Khalik, I'm here, and I'm real." Hassan confirmed after they hugged.

"Yeah, but how?" Khalik asked once more.

Hassan lay unconscious on Chavez's basement floor; the smell of the smoke in the air from the burned-out fire awakened him. Coughing and barely able to breathe, Hassan was in extreme pain from the burns to his body. He looked ' the room to see what was once Juan, but now just an unrecognizable body, smelling the room of burnt flesh. As he lay there looking at Juan's dead body, Hassan began to try to get loose from the rope that tied his hands.

He did not have to squirm too much because the rope had easily come loose from the fire that had been set upon him. The rope released from his wrist, and Hassan began to scoot along the floor to try to get to the basement door. When he finally reached, Hassan pulled his self up and rested his back up against the wall, trying to catch his breath. He was hurt and could barely move. His skin had been set ablaze and nearly charred in several places of his body.

If it hadn't been for the big bucket of water thrown onto him before being set a fire, he would probably be dead just like Juan, but that wasn't going to stop Hassan from getting free and getting his revenge. As he looked around, he noticed a small window that had been cracked open. The window was a bit high up, and he would need a chair just to get out of it. Hassan looked around the room and noticed an empty wine crate across the floor.

Now all I need to do is get myself up, He thought. Hassan began to try to pull his self up but kept falling back down. *O.k. if I do not pull up and get out of here they are going to find me and when they do, I'm dead.*

Late into the night and the smoke from the basement fire seeped from the vent into Chavez's room. By now, his wife had been so used to the smell over the years that it did not even bother her nor did it wake her. Chavez sat at the head of the exquisite dining room table that stretched halfway across the room. The two guards sat at the table as well, drowning themselves in the bottles of expensive wine that sit at the table, celebrating as they just accomplished another vengeful death.

Hassan finally pushed his self up from against the wall despite the pain he was feeling. He stood up and steadily began to take baby steps across the room, heading towards the wine crate across the floor. Hassan picked up the crate and grasped it tightly into his hand slowly walking over towards the window. He placed the crate on the ground and put one leg on top of it then grabbed a hold of the ledge outside the window to keep his balance before stepping all the way onto the crate. Hassan began to lift the window up, while standing on his tip-toes, and trying to maintain his balance. He struggled and pushed until he finally got it open. *"Damn, how am I gonna get out of this window?"I'm too weak.* He thought.

Hassan did not let that bother him. He placed both of his hands upon the window ledge and began to pull his self up. Finally, he could get his chest onto the window ledge, and he placed his hand outside of the window and grabbed a hold on the house to pull his self out even further.

Jazell stood outside on the balcony outside her bedroom crying. As the tears rolled down her cheek, she could smell the stench of smoke and death. The smell was faint but passed through her nostrils as the wind blew. She looked up from her head resting on the balcony rail-ing and began to look around. She looked down and could not believe what she was seeing. Someone was crawling from the basement win-dow. She gasped. *Oh my god.* She thought.

Jazell ran from the balcony outside her room and slowly opened up her bedroom door. She could hear her father and the guards down-stairs laughing. She knew that they were drunk by the sound of the tone to their voices. Jazell went out into the hallway and closed the door to her bedroom. As she walked through the hallway, she passed her mother and fathers room. The door was cracked. She could see that her mother was fast asleep. She began to walk down the hallway and slowly down the long stairs, hoping that no one would see her.

When she reached the bottom of the stairs, Jazell crept towards the foyer and then to the front door. She looked back and could see a glimpse of her father in the dining room. She knew that she only had a little of time to get out of the house. If her father found out, he would kill him, so she had to get to him first. Jazell noticed that the house alarm had not been set. If anyone wanted to kill, her father now would be the time to do so. She opened the door slightly and slid through, hoping that no one would hear her.

Hassan finally made it through the window and lay there resting on the ground from the fall. He was in pain and felt as if he could not go any longer when he looked up and seen someone standing over him. It was Jazell.

"Hassan how did you… I mean… I thought you were dead." Lovely expressed

Hassan looked at Jazell. "I told you can't anybody stop me baby." He said sarcastically.

Jazell kneeled down and lifted his head from the ground. She hugged him tightly "Oh baby I'm so glad that you're o.k.

"Ouch, be careful." Hassan said

"Oh I'm so sorry, baby. We have to get you out of here before my father finds you, and he will make sure that you are dead this time for sure." Jazell carefully lifted Hassan up by his arms and pulled him from the ground. She slowly walked him towards the side to the house and sat him in between the bushes that sit near so that no one would spot him. "Look, wait here and don't try to go anywhere. I will be right back. You just stay here and rest."

"Where are you going? You cannot leave me here like this. What if your dad comes back? He's gonna kill me for'sho." Hassan said to her grabbing her arm.

"You have to trust me. I will be back, don't worry, and just sit tight." She reassured him.

Jazell turned and walked off. She knew that she had to do something if she wanted to get away from this. She could not take it any longer, the constant controlling, no freedom, and most of all the killing. Jazell walked into the front door of the house and lightly closed it. She could still hear her father and the guards ranting and laughing at the table. She walked towards the living room and could see her father's jacket lying across the chair. His keys and his gun were sticking out from the pocket. She placed the keys in her bra. Jazell had never known her father to slip up like he has. She grabbed the gun out of the pocket and checked to see if it was loaded. There were four bullets into the chamber. She knew in that moment what she needed to do.

Chavez sat at the head on the table and raised his glass to make the last toast to his self, "A final toast to me, and my power."

The guards raised their glasses and joined in on the toast. "To power." They said slurring their words.

As Chavez took a sip, he could hear the sound like a click in his ear as Jazell cocked the gun and rested the barrel against his head. The guards were in awe. They were not sure if they should shoot now and ask questions later. Chavez did not move. He did not even act as if he was scared.

"Oh don't look so surprised fellas. Let us make that last toast to my father for all the killing, stealing, lying, and controlling things that he does. Let us toast to him for being a monstrous and heartless bastard. Go ahead daddy, make your toast." Jazell stood behind him with the gun against his head and wondered what he would do next.

"Well, well, well, my daughter has grown some balls," He said sarcastically, "I know you're mad right now about your little fling, but I assure you it was for the best. Now run on upstairs and go on to bed."

Jazell could feel his vengeance through her heart. It made her tremble inside. He was being too nice and patient in the situation. She had placed a gun against his head and all he could say is he knew she was mad. This was not good. Chavez dared anyone to cross him, or they would pay. He had no remorse for anything he had done, and she knew it. Jazell knew her father all too well, and if she did not kill him, first then he would get her as she slept.

She looked up and could see her father's face through the glass China hutch. He was signaling the guards to make a move. She looked over at the guards and could see one of them about to make their move and going for the gun in his back pocket. Jazell quickly reacted and grabbed her father by the throat, placing him into a headlock. As the guard drew his gun, she shot him in the chest and then fired a round into the other guard before he could make a move. They both lay there dead, killed instantly from one shot.

She let loose from the chokehold she had her father in and placed the gun back towards his head. "Now that you don't have your hired help. What are you going to do to your precious daughter, huh, how does it feel to be betrayed like you do everyone else?"

"Well done Jazell. I knew you would come around eventually. It is in your blood. Now you have proven your point so why don't you just put the gun down."

"You see daddy; I am in control now and you, well; you are still trying to manipulate me. I have the gun father, me!" She yelled out to him.

Chavez became angrier. "First it was cute of you to stand up for what you believed in, but now you're just being a stupid bitch. I have no tolerance for this kind of behavior Jazell, you know this. Now put the gun down for you regret it!" He yelled

"Bitch, Is that what I am to you father?" Chavez looked at her and smirked evilly. It made her more furious, "Have fun in hell because that's where you belong you heartless bastard." She fired at her father until there were no more bullets left. Her nightgown drenched in blood.

Jazell ran up the stairs to wash up quickly and get a fresh change of clothes. Running past, she could still see her mother fast asleep in the bedroom. She walked in and walked towards the safe next to the bed. There on the nightstand she noticed a bottle of pills, and one opened lying next to her. The bottle was empty. *Mom*, She thought as she checked for her pulse, but she knew that she was gone. Her skin began to get pale and slightly cold. *Oh mom*, tears began to flow from her eyes as she hugged her mother one last time. She did not have to wonder why because she knew of the pain and hurt already. Jazell got up from the bed and kneeled down to the safe, putting the password in. She knew that her father always kept stacks and stacks of money in the safe next to his bed. Although he had many of them, this was the only one that she could get access to. She reached onto the bed and grabbed the pillowcase from the pillow then placed the money from the safe into it. She filled it up, ran to her parents' closet, and grabbed a duffle bag to place the money in.

Hassan sat there wondering what was going on. He could hear the sounds of gunfire coming from the house. Just then, he saw Jazell. She carried a large black duffle bag and had changed into different clothing. Hassan needed not to ask her anything he could tell by the look from her eyes that she had just committed her first crime. She had a vengeful look on her face, with still a splatter of blood on her cheek.

Jazell ran to the car and opened up the trunk, placing the bag of money in it. She hurried back to Hassan, who had become speechless, and helped him to the car. She placed him in the backseat and carefully laid him down. "Wait here." It was the first thing she had said since she came from the house. Jazell ran back into the house and grabbed a tank of gasoline that her father kept in the garage. She went into the kitchen and grabbed a box of matches from the drawer. Jazell went into the room where her father and his guards lay upon the ground dead and began to pour the gasoline over their bodies. "Like I said have fun in hell," she said to his lifeless body as she lit the match and dropped it on his chest.

There was no time to waste. She ran out of the house and quickly got into the car, driving off as the house began to smoke and slowly burst into flames. Hassan was stunned. As Jazell sat there driving away she knew that there was no going back, and she had done it all for him.

"Wait a minute, how did you know I was getting out?" Khalik added to the long list of questions he had already asked.

"You'd be surprised what a lot of money can buy you. Anyway, fuck the small talk, I'm back, and we set for life." Hassan said with the most confidence in the world.

Khalik looked into his eyes. "Yeah"

"Yeah, I took care of all of that." Hassan assured him, and Khalik smiled "Aiight then let's get your ass away from here."

They walked back towards the car, and the windows began to roll down. There sitting in the front seat was Jazell and a stack of money into her lap.

She handed the stack to Khalik "Here this should help get you cleaned up for your new life."

Khalik looked at Jazell and then he looked at Hassan once again. There was no need for him to explain, he knew his boy and the look upon his face explained it all. It was priceless. They had set out to be some of the richest youngsters in Chicago, and they succeeded.

Jamel lay in the bed awakening from the small beam of light coming from the thick double pleaded and outdated floral curtains. His eyes squinted twice before opening them and wiping the crust from within the creases. As his bare feet hit the floor, he arose, letting out a loud yarn with the stench of his own morning breath when he heard a knock on the door.

Morning Paper, coming from the voice of the man on the other side opposite the door. Jamel walked over when he noticed the newspaper placed through the crack under the door. He picked up the morning edition of the Chicago Tribune when he noticed stamped on the front page were a picture and entire article printed on him and his escape from prison. He read further down the page *police are now linking several recent homicides from the Chicago area and a possible disappearance of one of their own, Detective Beau Whitman, to escapee Jamel Johnson.*

His hands felt limp as he dropped the paper onto the ground and paste the ugly brown carpet that was outdated and well overdue for a replacement. Jamel walked out towards the balcony and opened the sliding door. He stood there staring into the mornings' sunlight. *Man what in the hell are they talking about? Fuck, what have I gotten myself mixed up in?* He thought about the newspaper article on his escape and wondered why the police would be trying to connect him to the disappearance of Detective Whitman. He had no knowledge of his disappearance or his whereabouts. Still, he could not help to think about the deaths among the people he had been involved in.

Jamel lowered his head and placed his hands on his head with his fingers intertwined. He thought back to the love of his life, Chanel, and how after all these years of losing her only to find her and lose her again. And his daughter. The daughter he had never known about for all these years, and now she too was gone forever. He would not get her beautiful face out of his mind. How could he live with his self? With what he has done. He went from an escaped felon to a murderer all in the short time back on the streets. He had killed the only two people left in the world to carry down his name, his bloodline. And for this, he did not want to go on. Nevertheless, he had to. This was his chance to get his life back. His chance to start all over. To start fresh.